TYGERS

TYGERS

J. WARREN

New Orleans

Published in the United States of America and United Kingdom by
Queer Mojo
A Rebel Satori Imprint
www.rebelsatoripress.com

Paperback ISBN: 978-1-60864-172-7
Ebook ISBN: 978-1-60864-173-4

Library of Congress Control Number: 2021943013

The tygers of wrath are wiser than the horses of instruction.

The Proverbs of Hell
—William Blake

For George, who was so kind

For Sonja Ann, who asked

CHURCH ATTACK CLAIMED BY FRINGE GROUP

By Jennifer McMahon

September 20th, 2015

The brutal attack that killed 19 on Tuesday in a Catholic church on the East side was planned, says the terrorist group who has claimed responsibility for the bombing. The leader, speaking in a pre-recorded video released to the internet at the same time as it was delivered to several news agencies, said that there would be more attacks soon if changes weren't immediately made to laws restricting the lives of lesbians, gays, and the transgendered.

The video also confirms that the bombing of the church during a wedding ceremony between what the group termed as "a straight man and woman" was intentional. The fact that this was a Catholic church was also planned, the leader said. The group wants equality for LGBT people, and is using what one source called, "Fairly standard terrorist tactics."

An FBI spokesperson says that this group has claimed responsibility for several other attacks. It is believed that they were responsible for another bombing that occurred a year ago in Mississippi. He went on to say that the message mentioned what this fringe group said there had been a "war on gay people" for which the group blame President Thompson. "They seem to believe that since the President was elected, and now re-elected, this has given permission for conservative extremists to declare war on gay people," the source said.

The spokesperson also said that the bomber is unidentified at this time, but that witnesses reported seeing a very young man, possibly a teenager, walking across the street toward the church just before the explosion. There are unofficial reports that a young man with severe injuries who may be the bomber is in critical condition at Belle Reve hospital at this time. Whether or not he is expected to survive and what legal action may be taken against him if he is the bomber is unclear at this time. Chief of Police, Arnold Sower, said "It is our responsibility to make sure that extremists like this are stopped, and we take that duty very seriously. These men will be found, they will be stopped, and justice will prevail."

AARON

My name is Aaron.

In about two minutes, I'm going to push this red button.

Then, I'll explode.

I know that when a kid like me says that, what he usually means is that he feels stressed out about prom, or his parents are down on him about his grades. I know that's what you're thinking, even right now.

Thing is, though, you're wrong.

What I mean, as I walk up this last set of concrete steps outside this church, is that there is a vest with explosives strapped to my chest. In my right hand is a little round plastic handle that used to be on a toy of some kind. I know that because I can feel the jagged lip where the handle used to be joined to something. I can't stop my fingers from playing with it, the sharp edge cutting in to my fingers. It's the kind of thing that Marcus would find funny; using the handle of some toy gun to make a real trigger. On top of the trigger is a little button that, when I press it, will send a signal to the charges attached to this vest, and then I will explode.

I guess I'm a terrorist.

I know that when I say this, you're going to think, "He must be a Muslim." But I'm not. Not that there's anything wrong with being a Muslim. I remember Ahmed from pre-calc. He's a funny guy with a great smile. It's just I'm not one. I'm just some white kid from Arizona. I'm nothing, really. That is, until I push this button.

Then I will be something.

Last step. Now I'm standing outside the two enormous wooden

doors. Just to the right of them, there's a board with a lot of information on it. The name of the Priests, the scheduled events for the week, an inspirational Bible quote: "Revenge not yourselves, my dearly beloved; but give place unto wrath, for it is written: Revenge is mine, I will repay, saith the Lord" Rom 12:19. I guess that's ironic or something.

Back across the street, I know that Marcus and the rest of them are watching me, wondering why I've stopped. I want to keep going. I have to keep going. But my legs are jelly, and as I raise my hand to the long brass handle on the door, I am wondering what this is all about. Am I a terrorist? I mean, I guess because I decided to do this thing, there really is no going back. Richard said there was no way to take the vest off once it was on without blowing the charges. He said that was something he'd learned "over there," and as I'm standing there it only just now hits me that he meant somewhere like Iraq or Afghanistan or Northern Ireland. I should have asked him.

I'm watching as my hand pulls on the handle and the door opens. Inside an organ is just starting up. Ahead of me, across the little entry hall, a man in a tux is leading a woman in a long white dress through a doorway in to the main church. This is it. The moment. Marcus said it had to be now.

I walk up behind them as if it's the most natural thing in the world. I can't feel my legs. I'm about halfway down the aisle before anyone really notices that some stupid kid that no one recognizes is walking behind the bride. People are just starting to get that look on their faces that means they've decided to do something about it when I stop walking.

By this point the bride has stopped, and she's turning to look back at me. I just catch her eye, and she's got this look on her face—smiling with eyebrows close together, as if she is about to ask me something before I say I'm sorry, and then I press the button.

MARCUS

File 2618-69370-B
Index: 1-10:41
Room 1159B
Transcript follows:

Harper: Intake interview, prisoner 9370-B, Agents Bill Harper and Mary Ann Winn present. State your full name for the record.
(silence)

Harper: State your full name, please.
(silence)

Winn: Look, you can either answer this man's questions, or you can answer mine somewhere a bit more private. What's it going to be?
(silence)

Harper: The tough guy routine isn't going to do you any good, here. The sooner you cooperate, the sooner we can transfer you. Get you settled in somewhere with a bed and hot food.

Prisoner 9370-B (hereafter referred to as "prisoner"): Bullshit

Winn: What did you say, pal?

Harper: Whoa, there. Okay, turn it off.

Index: 1-15:74

Harper: Intake interview, prisoner 9370-B. Agent Bill Harper present. State your full name for the record, please.

Prisoner: Vladim Illych Petrovsky

Harper: Vladim, for the record, you have been charged with a number of crimes, not the least of which are first degree murder and several other crimes which fall under the category of terrorist actions.

(silence)

Harper: Vladim, I have to tell you, this tough guy routine you keep insisting on isn't going to get you anything but a world of hurt. Cooperate. Cooperate and we can get this all done and get you someplace settled.

Prisoner: (something garbled, perhaps in Russian).

Harper: What was that?

Prisoner: I said bullshit.

Harper: Why is that bullshit?

Prisoner: Unlisted flight, off the books airbases. Talk, don't talk, it doesn't matter. Dead is dead.

Harper: Vladim, I'm starting to feel like I'm not going to get anywhere with you today. That'd be alright, normally, except that I have a deadline to meet. You keep stonewalling me, and what's so funny?

Prisoner: That phrase. You use it like it means nothing.

Harper: What phrase? Stonewalling?

Prisoner: (something garbled, perhaps in Russian)

Harper: What was that?

Prisoner: Typical hetero idiot; you don't even know your own history. Read a book, you

(there is a loud bang and the sound of chairs scraping against concrete)

Harper: You were saying?
(someone spits)

Prisoner: June 1969.

Harper: What about it? That was the day we beat you to the moon.

Prisoner: (laughs) Aren't you little old to believe in fairy tales?

Harper: You are determined, aren't you. Okay. We'll talk tomorrow.

Index 2-08:37

Harper: Intake interview day 2, prisoner 9370-B, Agents Bill Harper and Mary Ann Winn present.

Winn: Jesus, they really fucking worked him over, huh? Can he still talk?

Harper: For their sake, he better be able to. Those apes. Can you still talk?

Prisoner: Yes.

Harper: Okay. Are you planning on being any more co-operative today?
(silence)

Winn: Look, Trotsky, you keep this up, and they're just going to keep on bangin' away on you like a drum solo. Fucking give us something.

Harper: Anything to start this off.

Prisoner: Is not storytime with Babushka. You want answer? Ask question. I tell or I don't tell.

Harper: Okay. We searched all the databases we have, and there is no one called Vladim Illych Petrovsky. Tell me your actual name.
(several minutes of quiet, then a scraping sound, likely a chair against concrete)

Prisoner: Or what? (transcriber's note: at this point, the voice has changed quality entirely and sounds British)

Winn: What the fuck?

Harper: Don't make me have to keep threatening you. It's getting old.

Winn: Fuckin' A

Prisoner: You won't find me in any of your databases, your files. What would be the point of anything I've done if all you had to do was fucking Google me?

Harper: Give me a name. That's all you have to do for today just give me a name and you can get a hot shower. Remember those?

Prisoner: Marcus.

Harper: Marcus what?

Prisoner: Just Marcus.

Harper: (exhales loudly) So you want me to go off and search everything I have for just one name?

Prisoner: You're the straight white male in the room aren't you the master of all you survey? (chuckles)

Winn: Laugh it up, buddy. I don't like your chances you keep fucking with us.

Prisoner: Who's fucking with you? You asked for a name, I gave you one. Are we done here?

AARON

"I wish I could be there to see their faces," one of the guys that I don't know says.

The corners of Viktor's mouth do that thing they do when he is annoyed.

I'm cold because I'm standing in this storage unit with my shirt off. Richard says he has to wire it to me right against my skin so that the bulk doesn't tip anyone off. He says too many guys get pinched (that's how he talks) before they can detonate because it's too obvious that they're wearing a vest. Just behind him, staring at me, is Marcus.

Viktor puts his hand on Marcus' shoulder, and I get mad. I mean, I know I'm about to die, but I don't want anyone else to be with Marcus but me. Even after I'm dead. I know how stupid that is, but there you go.

Marcus puts his hand on Viktor's shoulder, and they don't say anything. Then Viktor shouts "Let's go!" without looking away from Marcus, and five of the guys who've been standing around pick up guns and put them under their jackets, then follow Viktor out.

"Where are they going?" I ask Richard.

While he's still adjusting the wires around the vest he says, "They're going to set up the next phase. The next gig. Whatever they call it. I don't know what it is. They don't tell me in case something goes tits up. They're gonna' capitalize on what you're about to do, little man."

As soon as Viktor is gone, Marcus turns his attention back to me. It's so corny, I know, but when he does, I relax.

"How long?" he asks Richard.

"Not long now," Richard says, clicking something in to place underneath my armpit. I'm worried that I might be really sweaty under there, but I'm afraid to move.

Marcus walks around in front of me so that all I can see is him.

"Breathe," he says, smiling.

I laugh just a little, then remember the explosives being wired to my chest.

"You're so important to me. To this. To all of us. We're never going to forget you," he says. I just want his hand on me somewhere, but he's just outside how far I could reach with this vest on. Then he reaches out and puts his hand on my cheek. His eyes soften just a bit. "Generations of kids will remember your name. If they rebuild this church, two men might be able to get married here, and they'll remember you. They'll remember your sacrifice."

"How?" I ask, and I hate how my voice sounds like a bird chirp.

"Because I'll tell them. I'll make sure everyone remembers. Richard?"

"Almost there," Richard says as I hear another snap. "Just one more."

I want to tell him how afraid I am, but I'm afraid that if I tell him how afraid I am, he'll be disappointed in me. This is how I'm spending the last minutes of my life.

"So beautiful," Marcus says, and I just want to be naked, again, and next to him. I want his arm around me. "So brave," he says.

I know I'm shaking.

"There," Richard says, "just like a Christmas tree. Here," he says, and puts something in my hand. It's a black plastic handle with a black button on the top. A wire leads from it back to the vest. "When you get in the door, press the button, and kiss Saint Peter hello for me." He smiles, but in that way that means he's excited for something dangerous that's about to happen, not in a way that means he cares. This is fun for him, like strapping bottle rockets to the family pet on Fourth of July. He's the kind of guy no one wants to be around until they have something dangerous, like this, to do. Then everyone loves him. The worst part is, I think he knows it.

"Okay," I say.

Richard backs off a ways, wiping his hands on a dirty green towel.

I look back at Marcus. "Let's go," he says. He carefully puts my jacket over the top of the vest, and snaps each button slowly. His fingers brush over the stupid peace symbol patch I put on it a few months ago. That seems like some foreign country, now. A different life altogether. Some other kid who looks like me but isn't.

He snaps the last button and puts his hand between my shoulders. It comforts me, but I know that it's also so that if I try to run, he can keep me there. There are always two sides to everything that Marcus does. I know he loves me, but I know part of that love is that I'm willing to do this for him. I'm looking at the floor, watching each of my steps, and thinking about how dirty my shoes are.

"You're going to be remembered in the same breath as King, as Ghandi, as Guevara. A hero to the cause," he's says as we get closer to the door. I'm trying not to think about how two of those men did what they did peacefully, not through bombs. "You'll help us make them see that their war on us is no longer one sided. That they can't just keep lobotomizing us, imprisoning us, and killing us without consequences. They have to be shown that there are consequences."

"Yeah," I say, but it hardly comes out. We're at the door. We stop. He turns to face me again. He puts his hands on my shoulders.

"Today," he says, "you're a hero." He squeezes my shoulders, and all I want him to do is pull me to him and hold me. But I know he can't. The vest. "Go on, now," he says, "and make me proud."

He opens the door for me and pushes my shoulder just a little. I step out into the little hallway and walk to the glass door. Across the street, I can see the church with its big white spire. As I step out on to the sidewalk, I can see a taxi glide to a stop outside the church, and someone in a nice suit pay in a hurry, then run up the steps. As I step out on to the street, I'm thinking that whoever that guy is, he's going to wish he'd been just a bit more late. I guess that's funny.

MARCUS

File 2618-69370-B
Index: 3-09:53
Room 1159B
Transcript follows:

Harper: Intake interview day 3, prisoner 9370-B, Agents Bill Harper and Collin Washington present.

Washington: Jesus, he doesn't look so good.

Harper: Ever since he got here, he's been trying to act like a hardcase. Good morning,
Marcus. Turns out, you weren't bullshitting us. Deep web has all kinds of information about a person walking around with the name Marcus, no last name. (sounds of paper hitting a desk) This you?
(a long silence)

Prisoner: Turn the page, please?

Washington: You're kidding, right?
(the sound of paper moving, then more quiet)

Harper: Are these posts from you?

Prisoner: Who can tell?

Harper: You should be able to if you're telling us the truth. Are these your posts?

Prisoner: They would appear to be. But then they could be fakes.

Washington: I think I see why the guys keep tuning him up.

Harper: These documents have already been introduced into the case. This particular batch seems to be a conversation between someone calling themselves Marcus and another unidentified person. They seem to be discussing the assassination of Winston Mendez. Care to comment?

Prisoner: I didn't get to read all the way to the end.

Harper: This conversation seems to be about instructions for tracking down and killing the homosexual rights advocate Winston Mendez a month before Mendez was murdered during one of his public appearances. An appearance in a town, I might add, where these came from.
(the sound of more paper hitting the desk)

Harper: Care to comment?

(a few minutes of silence)

Prisoner: What are they?

Harper: These are sworn statements from people who were working at an apartment complex. They say you rented from them. This apartment complex was not all that far from where Mendez was murdered. Thoughts?

Prisoner: No receipts?

Harper: What?

Prisoner: I don't see any receipts, here. I'm guess if you had them you'd show them to me, and they aren't here. Are you telling me you're trying to place me at the scene using word of mouth?
(quiet for a minute)

Washington: Son of a

Harper: Look, Marcus. You were there. You were there on orders to assassinate Winston Mendez. What I want to know is from whom? That's the guy I'm interested in, Marcus. Give me that guy and your whole life becomes much easier.
(four minutes of silence)

Prisoner: Tacos.

Harper: What?

Prisoner: Tacos today. One of the guards mentioned it. Tacos for lunch today. That'll be nice.

Washington: Is he for real?

Harper: You disappoint me, Marcus.
Index 3-15:28

Prisoner: What an unexpected surprise.

Harper: Intake interview day 3, prisoner 9370-B, Agent Bill Harper present. Tell me about Viktor Kanza.

Prisoner: (long unintelligible utterance) (heavy movement in the chair)
Harper: Ah. So, I see we're getting somewhere. Good. Who is Viktor Kanza, Marcus?

Prisoner: Go fuck yourself! (someone spits)

Harper: He's not doing so great, Marcus, I have to tell you. He tried to act like a tough guy when we pulled him in and now?...well, now things are pretty complicated for him.

Prisoner: What did you do, you mother fucker?

Harper: I didn't do anything, Marcus. I was here with

you.

Prisoner: If he dies, I promise you

Harper: You promise me what, Marcus? Hmmm? What do you promise me? Because while you're here throwing threats at me, Viktor? He's not doing so hot. He needs a lot of help. And we can get him that help. We could. Or

Prisoner: Or what?

Harper: Or we could decide that there's no reason to help him. I mean, it would all depend.

Prisoner: On what?

Harper: How cooperative you become in the next ten minutes or so.

Prisoner: You'll save him?

Harper: I can't promise he'll pull through, Marcus. I'm not kidding he acted like a fool and tried to shoot his way out of a situation where he was out-gunned. He's he's not doing great. But, if you start to help me out, then I might help him out.

Prisoner: Tell me what you want to know.

Harper: You'll cooperate?

Prisoner: Yes! But you must help him.

Harper: Okay. Then let's start at the beginning. Who is Aaron Miller, and what connection does he have to the St. Augustine church bombing?
(Sound of door opening)

Unknown: Agent Harper? A word?

Harper: A little busy at the moment.
(quiet for a moment)

Harper: Alright (sound of chair moving)
(quiet extends for 14 minutes)

(sound of door opening)

Harper: (sound of chair moving) Okay. So, where were we? Ah. Okay. Tell me about Aaron Miller. Why was he your target?

the rest of this transcript has been redacted

AARON

Lots of people move in and out of apartments during June and July. If they have families, that's when the kids are out of school, so the move is easiest. When you live in a complex like the one my mom and I lived in after she divorced Dad, you see it every year. Moving vans become such a common thing that you hardly even notice them. Early one day a van comes up and then leaves later that afternoon. Then a horde of other trucks and people swarm into that apartment to clean it, and another van shows up the next day and leaves later that afternoon. "Like being at an airport," Mom said one time when I'd said something about it at dinner. I didn't quite know what she meant, but I get it now—shoving people in almost faster than others can leave.

That summer was no different.

There had been quite a number of new move-ins. Sometimes I would walk by during the move or just after to get a quick glimpse at who the new people were. I'd gotten curious about two apartments, though, that sat close together near the entrance to the complex. I'd seen vans pull up, leave, the swarm of people show up to clean them, but no new moving vans pull up the next day. It being summer, and with little else to do, I started to investigate.

Two enormous black battered SUVs pulled up the next day right around dinner time. I went home, ate, then went wandering around toward that area again only to find that the SUVs weren't there, any-more. From the back yard I heard the sound of someone inhaling and exhaling loudly. I stepped in close to the fence and peeked through to find a man wearing only loose pants standing still and making strange motions back and forth in the air. I watched him for a while; he was powerfully built with dark hair and an almost square face. Each motion caused his muscles to ripple, as if waves of energy were moving from his chest outward.

I hadn't thought about how close I'd gotten to the dust of the fence, though, because at that moment I sneezed. My head actually bounced off one of the wooden slats. I stepped back from the fence and turned to leave but it was too late. He had already opened the gate and was staring at me.

"Hello?" he asked in a raspy voice with an accent that I couldn't quite place.

"Umm...hi..." was all I managed.

He continued to stare at me, waiting for me to say something. When I couldn't think of anything else, I said, "I have to get going."

"Tai Chi," he said.

"What?"

"It's called Tai Chi. It's not actually called that, really, but that's what people tend to call it, I should say."

"Oh," I said, not really connecting what he meant. "Okay," I said, and walked on. I couldn't very well turn around and head back the direction of the apartment I shared with my mom, so I walked toward the front of the complex. I couldn't turn around to see if he was watching me go or not, either. Something told me he was.

It took me almost thirty minutes to walk all the way around the complex, past the low wall that divided the property from a huge vacant lot next to it, to the back entrance and then to the pool and my apartment. When I opened the door and walked in, my mom saw me drenched in sweat.

"Where've you been?" she asked with a grin.

"Just out for a walk," I said and went upstairs. I couldn't get out of my drenched clothes fast enough. Then I reached for the laptop and looked up Tai Chi.

MARCUS

File 2618-69370-B
Index: 4-07:58
Room 1159B
Transcript follows:

Harper: Good morning.

Prisoner: You promised that if I gave you answers you would tell me about Viktor.

Harper: Good, so you are starting to understand how this works. That's important. I need you to know your old life? The one you had before we got you? That's all over. From here on in, you are nothing more than the information you can provide me. But you have people outside, people you care about, people who have needs. You cooperate and I can get them what they need.

Prisoner: Tell me what is happening to him.

Harper: I don't have all the information, yet. I can tell you this, though it isn't great. You would be proud of him, though, I'm guessing, in your own way. He fought us very hard. I'm guessing that's probably something you taught him, yeah? Well, just to make sure you don't congratulate yourself too much, if he hadn't fought us so hard, he might not be in an ICU right now. Do you see? If you told him to fight back as hard as he did, then it's you who nearly got him killed. We're doing our best to keep him alive. Make sure you think that one through. (quiet for a moment) When I have more information, I will get it to you. Provided you keep cooperating. I have more questions.

Prisoner: Then ask them.

Harper: The organization you work for, what is the structure?

Prisoner: I don't understand what you mean.

Harper: Strike one. Two more and I walk, and you don't get to know anything more for a while. See how this is going to work?

Prisoner: But what if I actually do not know the answer to the question?

Harper: Questions like the ones I have? I guarantee you know. Now, again the structure.

Prisoner: (quiet for a moment) You would probably call them cells.

Harper: Autonomous or linked?

Prisoner: Both.
(quiet for a moment. Sounds of pen on paper)

Harper: Your particular group was it a lead group, or were you taking orders from outside.

Prisoner: There is no lead group. There are only groups active and groups not active at any given time.

Harper: (sounds of papers shuffling) Where do the orders come from?

Prisoner: I don't know.

Harper: Strike two.

Prisoner: I am not lying to you.

Harper: Well, see, I don't buy that. In any given group there are followers and a leader. Hell, give three little girls a room to play in and a leader will emerge. It's how people work. You? You don't strike me as a follower. Thing about leaders is that they tend to know a lot about what's going on, even if they don't tell the people who are following them. They keep power that way. So I'm guessing you know a lot more than you let on at any given moment.

Prisoner: So do you.

Harper: Where do the orders come from?

Prisoner: Where do yours come from? Executive Directive 51?

Harper: I'm going to lose patience with you in a moment. Where do the orders come from?

Prisoner: Has a date been set, yet? I've always been curious.

Harper: (sigh) You know that I'm about to walk out of that door and that means one of two things for you either they're going to come in here and haul you away, which you'll resist again, and then they'll beat the shit out of you, or you cooperate and then spend the next 24 to 36 hours sitting alone wondering what's happening to your friend. Why not cooperate? I can make things better for you, you know. I have that power.

Prisoner: I'm also curious about what happens once the order is given. The camps, I mean. ADEX to REX 84 to what? I mean, it's all public record did any of you honestly think that we don't know what you're doing?

Harper: What are you talking about?

Prisoner: Things that are obviously above your pay grade. Maybe I need to be talking to someone who actually has a fucking clue.
(the sound of an impact)

Harper: I don't know if you noticed or not, but you're a dumb faggot handcuffed to a chair in government custody. Maybe you ought to take that into consideration before you start talking.

Prisoner: (laughing) I might be a faggot (the sound of spitting) but who is the one who is really chained up here? If you're free, get up and walk out of this facility right now.

Harper: I have a job to do.

Prisoner: You see? They don't even have to chain you. You chain yourself.

Harper: We're done here.

Prisoner: ADEX to REX 84 to what? This is the question.
(Sound of a door opening)

Unknown: Agent Harper, step outside for a moment.
(scraping sound of chair moving) (sound of door clos-

ing)

end of transcript for that day

5-08:27

Harper: Good morning.

Prisoner: You found out something very important yesterday, didn't you?

Harper: I'll ask you again what do you know about the St. Augustine church bombing?

Prisoner: I mentioned a few simple words and someone from the main office comes running in here to take you away. What does that tell you?

Harper: What, if anything, do you know about the St. Augustine church bombing?

Prisoner: 600 facilities, 800 facilities, we may not have an exact count some of them are underground, you know but we know what you plan to use them for.

Harper: This is your last opportunity to tell me what I want to know.

Prisoner: You see? Two little words I mention and they tell you that I'm "uncooperative" and that if

I don't answer today, they will what "take care of the problem?"
(silence)

Harper: Are you or are you not going to tell me what you know about the bombing of St. Augustine church?

Prisoner: What happens when the man who roots into other people's secrets for a living finds out people have been keeping secrets from him?

Harper: I realize you think this is a joke, some paranoid conspiracy thing like a TV show or whatever, but

Prisoner: Ah, that's what they told you, then. Paranoia. Delusion. I'm almost insulted that they went with the old standbys. I would have hoped for something with at least a little originality to it.

Harper: But what you need to know is that you're in a very serious situation. Cooperation and information are the only things that are going to save you.

Prisoner: (scuffling sound and a groan as if someone leaned on a table) Let me tell you a little secret, Agent Harper it doesn't matter what I tell you or don't tell you, they will never let me leave this facility alive. I knew that the second I heard your siren. I'm ready to die for what I've done. Are you ready to live with what you've done?

Harper: We're done here.

Cross-referenced file #1-B-62081
Agent present: Colin Vikram
Room: 109-45B
(Filer please note the change of prisoner location)

Index: 5-09:38

Vikram: Good morning. My name is Special Agent Vikram.

Prisoner: You're not FBI. What is that?

Vikram: This will sting a bit (sound of cloth moving)

Prisoner: (sound of air sucked through teeth) What is this you're pumping into me?

Vikram: The IV? Nothing harmful. We're just making sure you get all the fluids you need.

Prisoner: I had wondered when my cooperation would become unnecessary.

Vikram: We're going to start off very simply this morning. What is your name?

Prisoner: We know that ADEX and REX 84 didn't go away, they simply changed names. We know that lesbians and gays have always been the targets. What do they call the program now? For a laugh, we used to sit around and try to figure out what idiotic name they'd given the program to hide it, but (the sound of retching). So what's it going to be? Tail number N4476S? Diego Garcia? (sound of retching)

Vikram: I apologize. One of the side effects is nausea. I take it that you're starting to feel that now?

Prisoner: Fuck you.

Vikram: As I said, we're going to start off fairly easy this morning. All I'm asking is for you to tell me your name.

Prisoner: Pavel Fucking Checkhov (retching sounds).

Vikram: Your name, please.

Prisoner: Anton Yelchin (more violent retching).

Vikram: Your name, please.

Prisoner: You will get nothing fuck you!

Vikram: Oh, I think we both know that isn't true at

all. What is your name?

Prisoner: (after several moments at this point, the voice sounds more loose, relaxed) Marcus Rudenko

Vikram: I'm going to ask you to repeat that. What is your name, please?

Prisoner: Marcus Rudenko

Vikram: Marcus, tell me what you know about the bombing of the St. Augustine church.

Prisoner: (almost too low to hear) no

Vikram: Tell me who Aaron Miller is, and what role he played in the bombing of St. Augustine church.

Prisoner: Go fuck yourself

Vikram: Okay. I didn't want to play it this way, but you aren't making very good choices.
(sound of the door opening then closing and someone coughs)

Prisoner: What the fuck is that?

Vikram: This is simply going to help you to relax. Transcriber please note code 2350.

end of recording for this session

File 2618-69370-B
Index: 5-13:28
Room 1159B
Transcript follows:

Harper: Should we wake him up?

Vikram: He'll come around in a minute.
(there is quiet for approximately 5 minutes)

Harper: I guess I don't get it.

Vikram: Get what?

Harper: Conspiracy nuts. I mean, like this asshole. He thinks we're trying to round up every gay person in the country and put them in a vault underground or something. I admit, I wouldn't mind that so much, but

Vikram: People like conspiracy theories.

Harper: Isn't that the truth. I just can't figure out why. I mean, me? I want to think I'm smarter than the average bear. So why would I think up all these people making smarter moves than me? Who gets comfort from inventing a boogeyman?

Vikram: Bigger picture than that. See, the smarter the person, the more they are likely to realize that there's no big plot going on. No big, bearded guy who is keeping track of everything, ready to punish all those that need it. No great scoreboard that will reward them. It's just empty

Harper: He's coming around

Vikram: Just nothing. That scares them. They see it, and they usually try to get onboard with something to help God, cocaine something. Nothing works. Those are the ones to worry about because they start trying to connect the dots. They want the universe to make sense and when they find out it doesn't, they start inventing ways to make it fit. A guy like this? He wants all the dots to mean something, so he connects them and boom shadow governments moving behind the scenes plotting his demise. Fucking pathetic when you think about it. It's a kind of fantasy, really look, I'm so important that a whole government is trying to eradicate me.

Harper: Only, we are.

Vikram: Only because of what he did after the paranoia set in. Like it or not, he probably shot a man in cold blood, and probably blew up a church with a wedding party in it. There could be more, too. They were already watching him. It's how they found him so early.

Harper: Self-fulfilling prophecy?

Vikram: You guessed it.
(groaning)

Harper: How many like him you figure are roaming around?

Vikram: We'll find them.

Harper: Is he going to wake up?

Vikram: I wonder if maybe they didn't get the dosage right.
Harper: He's no good if we turn him into a vegetable before he gives us any information.

AARON

"Aaron?" my mother called from downstairs.

I immediately stopped what I'd been doing for the last ten minutes or so, slam the lid of my laptop closed and shift my chest so that the computer slides onto the bed. At the same time as my thumbs hooked the top of my underwear, my fingers hooked my belt loops and in one motion slid my pants back up and then twisted myself on my side facing away from the door. I just managed to get my fly zipped and buttoned before she knocked on the bedroom door and opened it at the same time.

"Yeah?" I asked, turning only my head toward the door, hoping she'd think I was napping.

"Oh," she said, "We need to go," she said.

"Okay," I said without getting up.

She stood at the door for a second, waiting. It would be a minute or two before I could stand up without her being able to guess fairly accurately what had been going on, so I didn't say anything and also didn't move. She turned and walked back down the stairs. Once she was gone, I closed my eyes and exhaled. The number of near misses always grew during summer, but that one had been the closest yet.

Once things had calmed down, I stood up and slid into my shoes. I thought about opening the laptop and finishing the shut down, but if we were going for groceries, then I'd be with her, and she wouldn't be up in my room snooping, so I left it.

She was waiting by the door as I came down the stairs, and I could see in her eyes she was doing that thing she'd started doing lately:

measuring me. I should explain—in the last couple of months, I'd gone from a somewhat plump around the middle 5 foot even to 5 foot 5 and a half, with no signs of slowing down. And it hurt. My shoulders and elbows creaked every time I moved.

She turned and started back down the stairs, saying, "I swear to god, I think you've grown since you walked in the door." This made me happy, but also roll my eyes all at once. "Let's go get grocery shopping over with," she said. Not my favorite thing, but okay. She's lucky I hadn't gotten very far along; even I don't like how mean I get the few times she's interrupted me when I was close. Normally, twenty minutes would have been more than enough to take care of business, but for some reason, none of the models were doing anything for me, that day. So, off to the local store, and the ritual of hovering around the *Men's Health* magazines coming up with excuses to ask her to buy one, but eventually talking myself out of it for fear she'd know why I wanted it.

She clicked on the radio. In the last few months, she's gotten into listening to talk radio. I don't understand why, but it's her thing.

"...groups continue to call for the government to step up their attempts to stop the activities of these vigilante gangs. This while the perpetrators of several incidents nationwide are still at large. The latest victim, 12-year-old Alexei Hamlisch, a Vermont teen whose body was found in a church parking lot just a mile from his home. Investigators say the word 'fag' was carved into the boy's chest with a large blade. Hamlisch becomes the 29th young person believed to have been lured by these online groups that claim all homosexuals are pedophiles, then murdered. So far, no arrests have been made..."

I get sick to my stomach, but I can't say anything. I glanced over at Mom to see what she might say, but she just stared straight ahead.

I wondered what she was thinking. Did she agree? I started to picture what I might do if I was caught by a group like that.

"...In other news, President Thompson, now in his second year of his second term, met with conservative religious leaders from several faith-based groups to discuss his changes to education policy. Listeners may remember that Thompson's 'Out of Sight, Out of Mind' educational campaign, which banned all material alluding to sexuality and sex education in all schools nationwide, met with widespread criticism from women's and gay groups early on but was passed almost unanimously by the Republican controlled House and Senate. The bill is expected to pass next week's renewal vote..."

I could see my mom's lips are pulled tight, but she didn't say anything. I stopped looking over her way, and stare out the window.

"...in news from the heartland, today, parishioners in one Tennessee city have finished construction on what is believed to be the largest megachurch in the United States. Almost the same dimensions as Universal Studios, the church is intended to be part worship space, and also testament to God's grace shed upon this country, a spokesperson for the project said. The spokesperson declined to answer when asked how much the total cost of the project was. I'm Jennifer Walsh, and that's your news update. Stay tuned for more 'Reconciling Faith' after these messages..."

I tuned out.

Mom likes to make spaghetti and lasagna because she can divide it up into little containers and we eat on that all week, so we always spend a lot of time in the pasta aisle. I think she likes that so that she only has to cook once every four days or so. It's okay, I guess, if you like thin red sauce. I looked longingly at the other types of shells wondering if just once we could have something else when she turns to me and tries to push my bangs back. She did this twice, but left her hand in my hair the second time. I was stuck between happy that she was being affectionate and a little creeped out by it. Her eyes locked onto mine.

"You need a haircut," she said.

"I do not," I said, wishing she'd stop.

She took her hand away, but her eyes stayed locked. "You used to part it on the right. It looked so nice. Why don't you do that anymore?" she asked, trying to brush it into a part.

"Because I'm not twelve?" I say, moving away from her and shaking it back into place and then walking away. I go all the way to the end of the aisle and pretend to be interested in a jar of red sauce.

"I think the part made you look nice," she said.

She picked up a box of lasagna noodles and set them in the cart. I guess I know what we'll be having for the rest of the week.

As soon as we got back in the car, she exhaled and pressed the button. The engine snapped to life. We'd left the radio on, so talk radio was coming back on. Without even asking, I tapped number two to get music, instead. The slowly fading chords of a song I recognized, one of the most popular tunes out right now, were fading out. "...and that was Take The Wheel with their monster hit, 'Jesus is the Way.' I tell you, Sam, they're the hottest band in the country right now."

"They sure are," the other deejay said, "and I have to tell you, not only is their message on point, but have you seen Mary Jane, the lead singer?" and then he whistled.

The first deejay said, "I hear ya'. Coming up on 3, and I leave you in the capable hands of Mr. Dean White with the Family Friendly hour. God Bless."

"Thank you, sir," the other deejay said, and another song started up. I tuned it all out.

When we got home, the message light was flashing. I put groceries away and hoped. When my father's voice came out of the speaker instead of anyone else's, I closed my eyes and exhaled. Shit. She listened to him tell her that the payment was going to be late again this month, and that he's got to go lead a youth group camp somewhere. I put the jelly in the refrigerator, trying not to think about how he'll be spending the summer hanging out with lots of other kids my age when I haven't seen him in over a year. I don't look over to see her standing the way she always stands when she's listening to his messages: one hand on the desk, the other brushing at a strand of hair on her forehead that won't tuck behind her ear, head down.

Dinner was, of course, tense. Every time I used my spoon to help twirl the spaghetti noodles into a ball on my fork, the clinking sounds rang out too loud. I found myself zoning out through most of it, and Mom doesn't talk, either. I try not to think about what the table would look like to someone watching us from the outside. When I finished, I looked over and mom wasn't done yet.

Upstairs, I closed my door and exhaled. I flopped down onto my bed, ran my hands over the brushed metal of the laptop my father bought me. It was his first present to me after the divorce. Mom didn't know I heard her, but she described it to my aunt Jessie as a guilt gift. I opened the laptop and set it on my stomach, my fingers autopiloted themselves to YouTube, and I fell down the hole of the video bloggers that I love. It's easier to get lost in the videos of them recording their lives than to live in mine, especially the English ones. Their lives seemed so glamorous and easy; they're beautiful and always flying to Dubai for the weekend. One video led to another and another, led to a recommended video, led to watching all that person's vids, led to watching the contents of their friend's video blog, and the next time I looked at the clock, three hours passed, and the room went dark. My eyes hurt, and the battery is way down.

I know there are other gays out there who do this same thing, but they just make me feel worse. They're all even more glamorous, and beautiful, and all I can think is that I'll never meet anyone like that. I'll never be someone like that. They're always hosting rallies to protest the government's voting in the constitutional amendment to define marriage as only between one man and one woman. They all hang out together at amazing apartments in Los Angeles, and I can only watch for a little while. Besides, I've seen the hate in the comment section of the gay vlogs, and it makes me want to curl into a ball and disappear.

I close the lid, put the laptop on the floor, turn on my side, and go to sleep.

MARCUS

File 2618-69370-B
Index: 5-17:38
Room 1159B
Transcript follows:

5-17:38

Harper: Good, you're up.

Prisoner: What did you people do to me?

Harper: We already told you we have most of your group. Viktor Kanza and Ji Yoen

Prisoner: Tell me how they are.

Harper: You start telling me what I want to know, then we'll discuss

Prisoner: (sounds of heavy movement) Tell me!

Harper: Calm down, or I walk out of here right now, and you spend another 24 hours not knowing what's going on with your friends.

Prisoner: Fuck you.

Harper: Last warning.
(two minutes pass in silence)

Harper: Why this Aaron Miller kid? He was 16. What use could he have been to you?

Prisoner: (sound of a deep inhale and exhale) Initially, the operation had nothing to do with him. He wasn't the one we wanted.

Harper: Go on.

Prisoner: There was another boy who had just moved into how do you say (something in Russian)?

Harper: Apartment complex.

Prisoner: The boy we initially wanted for the operation made videos on YouTube.

Harper: You're kidding, right? What use could a couple of barely-able-to-drive boys have to your cause?

Prisoner: The first boy, he made videos about being gay, calling for understanding of being gay, asking people to be kind to gays.

Harper: Alright. This was (sounds of paper shuffling)

Daniel Young?

Prisoner: Yes.

Harper: Jesus. Both of these kids look like they're 8. Why? The rest of your group, they were all men. Young men, but men. I'm not understanding.

Prisoner: Your country, it hates gay people. Your last election, you re-elect this ancient man who gets votes because he says gay people are monsters, yes?

Harper: President Thompson, you mean?

Prisoner: He gets first term by saying gay people shouldn't get married. He gets second term by saying gay people shouldn't be allowed to teach or be near children. His vice president says gay men are pedophiles.

Harper: Wait, what does this have to do with you recruiting these two boys?

Prisoner: Is simple. If we want to make biggest impact, we take boys who look young, innocent, so your country sees their picture and says, "We care about these boys." Then we reveal they are gay.

Harper: Wait, Aaron Miller and Daniel Young they were gay?

Prisoner: (laughing)

Harper: (sounds of paper shuffling) Go on.

Prisoner: The rest is even more simple.

Harper: But if you wanted to turn Daniel Young into one of your extremists, how did it turn into Aaron Miller who was strapped with the explosives?

Prisoner: I would like for you to tell me how my people are, now.

Harper: In a minute. I want you to tell me more about how you decided to switch from one boy to the other.

Prisoner: I would like for you to tell me about Viktor, now. What did you do to him?

Harper: What did he do to himself, you mean. Doctors say he'll recover eventually, but to say he resisted would be to put it mildly.

6-08:56

Harper: Agents Harper and Schroeder present for this session.

Harper: Jesus, how many times are they going to whack him out like this?

Schroeder: This is the second time I've seen.

Harper: What's it say?

Schroeder: (paper shuffling) Apparently, he tried to get out again. This time he faked sick and then went into an all-out Bruce Lee style rampage. Tasered more than once, then put down. I don't know much about dosages, but that's a pretty big number.

Harper: What should we do?

Schroeder: Let's wait. He might come out of it maybe.

Harper: Did he the last time?

Schroeder: No. He just sat there and drooled for an hour before Vikram and I decided to give up on it. How far did you get yesterday?

Harper: Just like the parents told us, the kids were boyfriends, one of them made YouTube videos.

Schroeder: Did you go watch any of them?

Harper: No, did you?

Schroeder: Yeah. They were mostly harmless. I mean,

fag propaganda no doubt, but not in any way in this guy's league. Not conspiracy nuts, either. Shame what happened, even so.

Harper: Yeah. Still, how does a guy like this one know about REX84B? There are congressmen on the subcommittee that oversees that stuff that don't know some of the shit he was spouting off.

Schroeder: Fucking internet. So many of those idiots out there with their little blogs and shit just typing away whatever delusions come to their mind that eventually a few of them hit on the truth.
Harper: I don't think he's going to wake up. Y'know, we really should complain if they keep delaying us like this because they can't get their doses right, there's no telling how many of his people might make it out of the net.

Schroeder: Trust me, whoever we don't already have is already out of the country.

Harper: You think?

Schroeder: You saw how well armed these guys were how well trained. You can bet on at least one thing: they're not working alone.

AARON

"Why don't you go over to the vending machines and get us some sodas, and I'll order pizza?" she said, rubbing my shoulder. I'm sure the pizza place would let her buy a 2-liter of something, but I didn't question the request; she never allowed sodas in the house, and so I knew this was a special thing. I had my coat on and was out the door before she even picked up the phone.

As I came around the last corner, my hand already reaching for the handle to the door to the tiny laundry room where the vending machines were, I nearly ran headfirst into the man who'd been moving in a week ago, the Tai Chi guy. He stopped for a moment, his hands in his coat pockets moving. Then he reached out and opened the door for me. I noticed that his knuckles were huge, and the skin on his hands dry.

I walked in through the door, knowing I should say thank you, but unable to look up from the floor. With a shirt and a jacket on, and in his thick-soled workman's boots, he looked much different than that first day. With the muscle and scars covered up, he somehow looked more dangerous than before. It was under those fluorescent lights that I noticed his eyes were dark brown.

He came in after me, letting the door close itself. I walked to one of the machines that had drinks in it, for a second forgetting why I was there. I could feel him looking at me. He was waiting for the exact same machine. My fingers were shaking a bit, and some part of my brain wondered why. After all, lots of people lived in this complex. I knew almost none of them, and yet they were constantly around. I'd even been in this exact situation lots of times; an adult waiting to use some piece of equipment I was using at the time never made me shake. None of them made me feel this nervous when I was near them. To make it worse, I was thinking about him watching me instead of putting money in and making a selection. The machine only had six rectangular buttons; six choices, and I'd already spent two- or three-minutes staring at them.

I made myself put in the money and hit the bright orange button, and the blue and white one. The machine thumped to life, something inside grinding, and then there was a single thunk. I lifted the orange drink out of the tray, expecting to hear a second thunk, but none came. As it had done a million times before, the machine only delivered the first drink. On any other day, at any other time, I could have told you that it was so old that it couldn't handle more than one thing at a time. I couldn't count for you the number of times I had warned little kids about the very thing that I'd gone and done; put in more than one drink's worth of money and tried to get more than one drink in a single go. Even as I was thinking this, I tried the thing that everyone tries, but has never worked in the history of mankind—the lever to return the the change.

The whole time, I wasn't mad that this was happening; I was mad for forgetting, and I was mad for looking like an idiot in front of this man. At the time, I couldn't have told you why, but I wanted to be cool in front of him. To look like a kid who knew what he was doing.

On the third pull of the change release lever, I leaned my head against the machine and said, "shit." Mom had only sent me with enough change for the two.

"Here," he said, a tiny clip to the end of the word that said there was an accent, but so little of one I couldn't identify it. His enormous hand was on my shoulder, and the other one slid about halfway back on the side. "Sometimes, you just have to be forceful." A huge bang happened, and then another, then a loud thunk as the other drink I'd ordered flopped into the tray. I was amazed for several reason, not the least of which was that there was less than three inches of space between this machine and the one next to it. He'd managed to generate that much force in such a small space. "There," he said, his hand squeezing my shoulder a bit before he let go.

"Thank you," I said, without moving.

He smiled, and I had to stop myself from saying something about it. "Excuse me," he said.

"Excuse...?" I said, then realized I was still standing in front of the machine. I backed up. "Oh," I said, "sure." I turned and walked for the door.

"Don't forget this," he said, holding out the can. I was mortified, but I knew I was supposed to smile and say something before I could walk very fast without appearing to be trying to get away from him.

"Thanks," I said, smiling, turning on my heel and leaving. I don't know if he was actually watching me, but I knew that it felt like everyone, the entire world, was. That they were all laughing at me.

One side of the apartment complex bordered on an empty lot. It was a huge area of uncleared land, just sand and bushes and snake holes and whatever. Next to that was a road built to lead to a cul de sac. No homes had been built on the cul de sac at that point, though, so it was empty. Beyond that was another uncleared lot. Just beyond that was the on ramp/overpass/off ramp of the highway. I liked to go to the wall that separated the complex from that lonely landscape sometimes, especially around dusk. I liked to sit down on that low wall and pretend I was the only person left in the world, sometimes. Or that I was staring at the surface of the moon.

I came around the corner that time, though, and there was a boy already there. I didn't know his name and had only a vague recollection of seeing him with one of the moving vans a week or so earlier.

He had one leg up, his chin resting on his knee. He saw me just as I saw him, and he raised his hand a bit from his lap without saying anything. At that moment, I thought I was breathless because I was surprised, but in that first moment he'd already taken my breath away.

I sat down next to him. For a second, I worried that I was too close, but he didn't move or say anything about it.

"It's kind of pretty," he said, looking out toward the empty.

"Yeah," I said.

He had one ear bud in and the other just dangling. On the screen of his phone was a boy who looked mad and quiet and sad all at the same time.

"Who are you listening to?" I asked.

"Hmm?" he asked, his eyes focusing on me for the first time.

"Who?" I said, pointing toward his phone.

"U2. Do you know them?" he asked. Something in his tone said this was a more important question than it seemed.

"Sure. It's a beautiful day or whatever," I answered.

He shook his head, "No. That's who they are now. They were different when they first started. Here," he said, and took the other ear bud, the one that had been in his lap, and held it out for me.

I took it, playing like it was no big deal, but touching that cord that was so connected to him, and then putting it in my ear—it felt important. "Listen to this one," he said. He swiped a few times, and the picture became what looked like a castle, and the color went from black and white to a pinkish. The song started playing, and he's right—it's nothing like the music I've heard on the radio. It's urgent, alive. The singer is singing about someone's eyes being as black as coals, and I look over to see that Daniel's eyes are closed. His chin moves just a bit, and I realized that the boy was singing along without opening his mouth. His little jaw movements matched perfectly with the words until, for that tiny moment, he was the one who was singing. His voice and the singer's voice were one and the same. His shoulders move in tiny jerks with the driving beat, and it's like the song is his heartbeat. I look at the small crease in his skin around his neck when I realize that his eyes are open, now, and he's looking at me. The song ends with us locked like that.

"See?" he said, "They were a lot different then."

The next song started with what sound like bells ringing out and echoing. For some reason, I couldn't take the closeness, though, and I took the ear bud out. I handed it back to him, and his fingers curled around it in my palm. He waited just a moment before taking it.

"Yeah," I said. Inside, all I want is to get away, or kiss him, or tell him everything I've ever wanted to say to someone else, or never see him again. My heart pounding so hard I know, I just know he could hear it. That he knows what I want, and don't want, or do.

I stood up. "I should get going," I said.

"You should come over some time where I can play you their early records."

"Yeah," I said.

"Okay. Saturday."

"Yeah," I said, getting on my bike, everything in my skull screaming *get away get away get away get away before he sees before he knows get away.* "Bye," I said quickly, already walking away.

"Bye," I heard him say behind me.

I don't like doing this. Let me say that upfront. It's stealing; and stealing from a band that Daniel loves. That's double not okay. But if I borrow Mom's card to download the songs, because I don't have a bank account of my own, she'll ask what I'm downloading, as she always does, and somehow, she'll know. Somehow, she'll just know.

So, this is the only way.

The library isn't very crowded, so I could get right to the CD case. No one ever bothered to alphabetize any of the CDs, so it took a while to find anything by them. They leave little post-it notes all over the case so you can take one, write down the shelf and space number you want, then give it to one of the librarians. Even this feels like an invasion. Somehow, they'll know. They just will, I know it.

When I saw the right album, though, I stopped. To anyone else, it would be just an old CD from a band their parents listen to, I bet. But to me, it was him. I jotted the letter and number down quickly. Then I rushed to the old woman behind the counter. She's helping a little kid check out his books while his mom and older sister watch. It'd be cute, but I'm seriously sweating bullets.

They finally finish, and she smiled at me as I step up. "Yes?" she asked.

I handed her the scrap of paper, barely whispering, "This one, please."

She smiled the obligatory "I wish you kids would read more" smile, then took her keys over to the CD case. She pulled out the one I want, the purple-ish one, and then another one just behind it. It was black and gray.

"Here you go," she said, setting the purple-ish one down, "and there was also this one just behind it—would you like that one, too?" she asked. It's the same band, and something about the title grabs my attention: *The Joshua Tree*.

"Okay," I said. I handed her my card and while she was scanning it and the CDs, I glanced around. It felt like everyone was watching me, and they all knew. The books they were reading barely disguised their smirks.

As soon as she hands the music to me, I bolted for the door.

"Young man!" she yelled.

I stopped, just knowing she was going to say something terrible because she knew. I turned around and she was holding my card toward me.

I walked back, mumbled thanks, took my card, and left even faster than before.

For some reason, just before I walked in the door, I tucked the CDs up under my hoodie. I don't want Mom to see them. As if she'd be able to, with one look, see what was going on. The door was unlocked so I knew she was home. The radio was on in the kitchen as I closed the door.

"I'm home," I yelled, already a quarter of the way up the steps.

"Okay," she yelled, and there was a loud hiss from something she was cooking. "Dinner's in about an hour," I heard her yell just as my bedroom door closed.

I heeled out of my shoes and collapsed onto the bed. I opened the lid to my laptop and fumbled one of the CDs into the slot. I grabbed the headphones from the headboard above me where I always keep them. I got them clicked into place and closed my eyes just as the first song started up.

It was like nothing I've heard before. See, I'm not really a music person. I know the stereotype is that all teenagers spend all day doing nothing but listening to music, but I don't. Music has just never really been that important to me. It certainly doesn't sound anything like the music on the radio, all full of twangy guitars and wholesome lyrics about trucks and Jesus.

The sound was immediately about loneliness, longing, but with a driving bass that makes it all feel so urgent. Then the voice came in, piercing. The image of a sword sliding delicately straight through to my heart. The breaks between the songs don't feel like full stops, but more like a slight pause for breath before continuing on with the same idea in a different way. I wanted to open the laptop all the way, fire up a search engine, and find out more about this band immediately, but I couldn't pull myself away.

The song that he let me listen to came on, and I immediately thought of him. How scuffed up his shoes were. I remembered him mouthing the words without opening his lips and, again, his voice became the voice of the singer. I remembered his tiny shoulder movements, and how thin his shoulders were. I started to think about what it would have been like to wrap my arms around them. To slide in behind him, wrap my arms around his, and pull him to me. The way his hair might have smelled up against my chin. How my hands would have felt against his stomach, both of us, eyes closed, listening to the same song.

I was just starting to feel some movements in my pants when, the next thing I knew, my mom is touching my arm. Startled, I pull one ear bud out. "Dinner," she said, her head cocked to the side a bit.

"Okay," I said.

I can tell she wanted to ask more but thought better of it. She glanced sidelong at me, turned, and left. I pressed stop, and the laptop is prompted me: would I like to scan the CD into my library? Some part of me understands that this is about more than just that question. Was I going to accept this music into me, to live with? I clicked "yes" and then pulled the other ear bud out.

At the table, Mom was quiet.

"Do you know the band U2?" I asked, still feeling some of the hesitation I had earlier. I felt like she'd know immediately why I was asking, but I also want to know from someone rather than just looking it up on a website.

"They're sort of old. From when I was your age. Why?"

I didn't know what to say. "Just curious," I said.

She looked at me for a moment, then started rolling her noodles up in a ball to take another bite. "Your father hated them. Said they were the most overrated band ever. He thinks that the lead singer…what was his name? Bomb-oh? Bondo? No, that's not it. I can't remember, but your father always said he hated that the lead singer thought he was some kind of savior. A 'naked messiah complex' he said, but between you and me, I think that was something someone else said that he was copycatting," she said, smiling to herself at getting a dig in.

"Oh," I said, pretending I knew what she meant.

"Where did you hear about them?" she asked, eating.

"Some people at school a while back," I said, eating.

"Are they still around? The band, I mean."

"Yeah."

She nodded a bit, a quirk at one end of her mouth.

"What?" I asked.

"I dunno; it's just…it's interesting to see what comes back around and what doesn't. U2. I would have thought some of the other bands that we thought were more cool back then might be the ones you guys would rediscover or whatever."

I shrug. I am glad on some level that she hasn't tried to find out more about it, but some part of me recognizes that she also didn't say what she thought. "What…um, what about you? What do you think of them?"

"Oh, I dunno. Your father was always the musical one. I just like whatever is on the radio, really. Well, mostly. I'm not really sure what's going on these days. It all seems to be very...I dunno...preachy, these days," she said, and took another bite. For a moment, there is only the sound of forks clinking on plates. I shrugged. "I remember, though," she continued after a minute, "that they had this one song about Martin Luther King. I can't remember the title, but I remember thinking how cool that was—that a rock band would take time to talk about something more than just getting to second base with a girl or whatever," she said, laughing. I smiled, too, even though I have no idea what "second base" meant. "Do...um, do you want to use my card to get some of their songs from the internet?"

In that moment, I did, but I also knew that if I did that, she'd want to talk about this again, and if we did that, I knew, I *knew* that she'd start to figure out what was going on. "No, that's okay," I said.

She nodded. It got quiet, and I felt bad. It's not that I didn't want to talk to her, I was just so afraid that she'd start asking the right questions, and then I'd say what I feared to be the truth and then what? What happened if she rejected me, called me disgusting? I'd heard the guys on the radio talk about the reprogramming camps for kids like me. When I could convince myself to get up the courage to read them, I've read the Tumblr posts about gay teens kidnapped with their parents' permission and taken to Puerto Rico or some place to pray away the thoughts or be beaten up. I knew the three letter word, but I couldn't say it. I couldn't even think it.

I swallowed the last bite, "May I be excused?"

"Yeah. I'll do dishes, tonight," she said, even though it was my night.

"Ok," I said. I mean, I wanted to say "thank you," but I've got so much going on in my head that it's all I could do just to get the plate in the sink and get back upstairs without breaking anything. I didn't turn the light on as I closed the door. The only light coming in through the window slowly fading from dark blue to black.

The laptop was finished moving the songs to my library, and I pulled the disc out, placing it back into its case. I put the other one, the one called *The Joshua Tree,* in. I lay the laptop on my stomach and stretch out, and put the earbuds back in. This one is even more lonely; it sounds like the music is echoing to me from somewhere far away. The bass is less urgent and sounds more like someone humming along with the song, like they already know it. I looked at the pictures in the little booklet—they all seem so smart, so earnest. Bono is the singer's name, it says. He was singing about not being able to find what he's been looking for, and for some reason, my chest clutched, and my eyes watered. I thought about the boy sitting on the low wall at the end of the complex. I thought about his fingers. About how one had a scar near the knuckle. As one song bled into the next to the next, I just kept thinking about how I could smell whatever laundry soap his mom used as we were so close. I remembered him singing without opening his mouth, and his voice blends with the singer's. For a moment, he and I are standing in a vast desert together, and he is singing to me.

Again, the laptop is prompted me: would you like to add this to your library?

I clicked yes.

VIKTOR

Marcus has this thing about feet. He loves them. I've never understood it, but if you could see his face when he's washing and massaging one of our sets of feet…it's like he finally finds peace. I like men's bodies, but there are certain parts of them that I put up with in order to get to the ones that I want. Marcus, though; he likes all of it, even the parts the rest of us don't really enjoy. It's especially uncomfortable for some of the younger ones who've never been worshipped like that. They expect that Marcus will be all brutal and domineering, but that's not him. He's not our leader because he believes that he is somehow better than us. He's our leader because he truly believes that the only way to keep us safe is by making sure we all do as he says. When we're safe, he takes care of us.

A night came where, after he and I had our sparring time training the younger ones, they all went off to the other rooms, and he and I were left alone. I didn't know it at the time, but I would come to think of this as the night before the party where he finally brought Aaron Miller into our group.

"Come on," Marcus said, and put his arm around my waist for a second. I would have followed him anywhere even without the touch, so I followed without asking. We both went into the apartment's bathroom, and he closed the door behind us. He turned the shower on, then put his hands on my hips. He moved me to sit on the edge of the tub. Warm air came up from under the shower curtain and floated over my back.

Marcus knelt between my legs and massaged my instep and kissed my ankle, then the same on the other foot. I won't go into all that he did after that, and I know that most people wouldn't find this kind of thing sexy at all—I would be one of those people, normally—but you have to understand: it's Marcus. Watching the calm and intensity on his face while he worshipped parts of me that I normally wouldn't even want to look at as if they were sacred to him left me feeling so connected to him, so aroused, that I could hardly breathe.

After he turned his attention to the rest of me, and we were both lying exhausted on the tiles, he smiled, took my hand, and lead me into the shower. He'd gotten the temperature just right without even looking. Then he washed me. Again, the calm intensity on his face was mesmerizing.

"What is it?" I asked.

"You are so important to me," he whispered, brushing my hair back behind my ear. "Things are moving very quickly, and I wanted us to have this time to look back on if things go...wrong."

"They won't," I said, taking his wrists.

"They might," he said, looking away from me. When he looked back into my eyes, I felt the same shiver I had all those years ago when he'd first taken me. "You have to promise me something," he whispered.

"Anything," I said.

He put his hands on my lower back and pulled me to him, his lips against my ear. "You must survive. Even if they catch you. Give me up, give up any of the others—you must survive. Promise me," he said. Then he leaned back and looked into my eyes again.

I have to say that, in that moment, I didn't know what to do. An unspoken rule we all had was that if we were caught, we should never give any information. Of course, the organization of the groups made it so that we knew very little, anyway, but any information in the right hands could jeopardize the entire mission.

"Promise me," he said, again, pressing me even tighter.

"I promise," I said, and he leaned in, making our embrace a hug. As odd as it sounds, something about the fact that we were hugging was more intimate than anything else we'd done that evening. "I promise," I said again. He put his hand against the back of my head and the other on the small of my back, then leaned back a bit so that he could see my eyes. "I promise," I whispered.

I'm thinking about all of this as the bullets destroy everything around me. The desk I turned over in a hurry to find some cover, any cover at all, would last maybe another five minutes at best. I could hear their boots, as well, between shots, always moving forward. As I'd been taught to do, I checked for any kind of exit from the room one more time. The only thing was a tiny window about seven feet off the ground far enough from the desk I was crouched behind that I'd never make it, even if I was one of the younger, smaller ones. Ejecting the clip showed one bullet left. I jammed the clip back in and thumbed the slide lock, gaining a tiny bit of courage from the click of the slide hitting home.

"I'm sorry," I said, seeing his eyes in front of me.

I stood up and swung the gun around. At least one of them was going with me.

MARCUS

File 2618-69370-B
Index: 7-09:26
Room 1159B
Transcript follows:

Prisoner: You said that you would tell me how Viktor was doing.

Harper: I did. The good news is that he's come through all of the surgeries okay. He is stable, but in critical condition.

Prisoner: What does that mean?

Harper: It means that he's very bad off, but that no new problems are developing at this time. At least, not last time I checked. Who knows, really? He's under heavy sedation and not really responsive enough to talk to at the moment. He was someone special to you. (sounds of paper moving) Your friend Viktor, I have to tell you he's got the boys upstairs scratching their heads. Maybe you can help us fill in some blanks.

Prisoner: Why should I help you?

Harper: Let's not go back through this again. Cooperate and things go well for him. You understand what I mean.

Prisoner: What has the mighty FBI so confused?

Harper: Kanza. That's fairly commonly Syrian. But the documents he had on his person were all written in Russian. Viktor is a much more Russian name than Syrian. So we figure he's from one of the families that stuck around in Syria around the time of the uprising, or maybe from a business family that came after.

Prisoner: (quiet for a moment) And?

Harper: Hoping you can tell us which, and why a man who is fairly obviously not ethnically Syrian has a somewhat common Syrian last name. I'm guessing when he wakes up, he's going to talk to us in Russian, am I right?

Prisoner: Dah (phonetic approximation inserted)

Harper: That why you two were close? Despite the British accent, we know you're Russian by birth, too. The guys over at Langley say most Russians who get a formal education wind up speaking with something that sounds like an upper class British accent. We figure that explains you. You both being Russian, though that why you and Viktor were close? He your boyfriend?

Prisoner: Contrary to what you might think, Agent Harper, I don't have sex with people simply because of their country of origin.

Harper: So explain Viktor to me, then.

Prisoner: Every nation rejects us, so we form our own. Where he came from is of no importance, really. It is what he does that matters.

Harper: Yeah, yeah, the glory of the cause, etcetera. Still, though, give me something. Before he joined up, was your friend coming out of Syria or Russia? Help me help him.
(almost two minutes of silence)

Prisoner: The family that gave birth to him moved to Syria from Russia so that the father could advise the government there how to use equipment that they had purchased from the company he worked for. They were living there before the uprising occurred.

Harper: See? That wasn't so hard. Why then the Syrian last name?

Prisoner: The father was killed, the mother was stranded and remarried. They changed his last name.
Harper: (whistles) Not an easy thing to do. Any idea

what the last name was before the change?

Prisoner: No.

Harper: Come on. Seriously, help us out here.

Prisoner: I honestly do not know it.

Harper: Listen, you've been a big help today, and I appreciate it.

Index 14:25

Harper: Hello.

Prisoner: Agent Harper. To what do I owe the pleasure?

Harper: I'd like to talk about the operation to kill Winston Mendez.

Prisoner: Ah.

Harper: We know it was you. Here's what I don't understand. If you and your group are some kind of I'm not sure gay crusaders for justice or whatever why would you want to off the guy who is doing the most to get the gay lifestyle choice accepted by mainstream straight folks?

Prisoner: How can I even talk to you about it when that's how you think?

Harper: When what is how I think?

Prisoner: "Gay lifestyle choice." If you could hear how fucking stupid you sound

Harper: Uh uh. Remember, I can just as easily clam up about how your friend is doing. I don't have to tell you anything about him. How about we keep things nice and civil.

Prisoner: I'm trying to answer your question.

Harper: How about we do it remembering manners, then.

Prisoner: It has to do with assimilationist thinking.

Harper: Explain that to me.

Prisoner: I'd really like a glass of water.
Harper: After. Tell me what you mean.

Prisoner: (sound of a loud exhale) You have a house, I'm guessing. You don't take your ring off before coming in here, so I know you're married. Therefore, house. Maybe, what, three bedrooms, one and a half bath? Nice sized back yard. Propane barbecue grill. Pool?

Harper: Yeah, so?

Prisoner: How much do you know about your neighbors? About the people the next street over? Let me guess not much. But you live next to them and feel comfortable. Why? What would make you feel comfortable living next to people you don't even know? The answer is lawn care.

Harper: What?

Prisoner: Lawn care. You feel comfortable around them because they keep their lawn neat. Tidy. They put their trash out the same day you do. They have a car that looks something like yours. Their kids dress similarly to your kids. Am I getting close?

Harper: Go on.

Prisoner: And when someone new moves into the neighborhood, can't you tell almost immediately if they are going to "fit in" or not?

Harper: Let's say you're right, let's say I can what does that have to do with what we're talking about?

Prisoner: You can tell whether or not they are going to fit in because you see it. If they want to fit, they'll start adapting almost immediately. If they don't, if they become the "weird family" on the block, everyone starts to dislike them. Now, ask yourself this does it have anything to do with who they are? No. Likely, none of you have even met them. You start to dislike them because they don't show signs of wanting to fit in. That's what makes you trust those others. Not that they dress the same or drive the same car, but that by doing those things you see that they want to fit in. To assimilate. You trust them because they have shown that they want to join the herd by becoming like the herd.

Harper: Okay, you scored a point. Down with the suburbs. So what?

Prisoner: Within any group of outsiders there are those who want to join the main group. Those who are only part of the outside group because of circumstance. Those who would rejoin the herd at a moment's notice if they had the opportunity. They desperately want to assimilate and would if they only had the chance.

Harper: What's wrong with that?

Prisoner: It gives power to the herd. You see, the goal shouldn't be for us all to be one gray, amorphous blob of sameness. The goal should be for us all to be different but to respect those differences.

Harper: And you're saying we don't?

Prisoner: In order for you to even understand what being homosexual is like, you have to put it in terms you understand. Choice, you remember? Choice, because you remember the time in summer camp when your best friend and you were swimming and for just a few moments the wrestling turned into something else and

Harper: Shut the fuck up.

Prisoner: Now who is forgetting his manners?

Harper: I'm not gay. I could never be gay.

Prisoner: No doubt correct. And yet there is that one troublesome incident, is there not? Maybe more? You convinced yourself that it was just because there weren't any girls around. You surrounded yourself with girls from that point on. You decided never to go down that road again. And for the most part you haven't. Congratulations you're a healthy heterosexual male. But because this was your experience of same sex attraction something almost all males experience during early puberty, by the way you assume that at some point I had the same opportunity for choice. I assure you, I did not.

Harper: So you gays keep saying.

Prisoner: Given how many of us are saying it, wouldn't that seem to suggest truth? At any rate, some outsiders will do anything if given the opportunity to assimilate back into the herd, as we discussed. Even accept however the herd wishes to think about them. So, rather than saying, "I am not as you imagine me to be," they instead say, "I'll be what you want me to be no matter how contradictory it might seem so long as you let me back in." And the herd, it very much likes this message. So, to those outsiders who show that they are willing to accept whatever terms the herd is willing to give, the herd shines its favor. Assimilationist messages gain a great deal of momentum.

Harper: And you're suggesting that this Winston Mendez was an assimilationist?

Prisoner: Yes.

Harper: That still doesn't explain why you'd want to kill him.

Prisoner: Agent Harper, to those who have no intention of surrendering to the herd, nothing is more dangerous than those who wish to assimilate at all costs. How can one ever make the argument that difference must be respected when the herd has only to point to those who say they do not want to be different? This would immediately destroy any chance of having the herd recognize difference as vital and important.

AARON

I lost count of how many times I walked around the complex each day going near the wall but not directly to it. "It's nice to see you get out more," Mom said. "I was beginning to think you were going to wind up merging with that computer, somehow."

After four difficult, antsy, angsty days, I found him sitting on the wall, again. His knee was up against his chin, and he was dangling his other leg off the low wall, his earphones in. It took fifteen minutes of psyching myself up before I could move from the corner I was hiding behind and come up to him. The whole time my heart was pounding. About halfway from my hiding spot to where he was sitting, I stopped for a second, and thought I'd turn around and go home to maybe try some other time, but he saw me out of the corner of his eye.

He waved—that tiny little gesture again—and suddenly I didn't want to run away anymore. I sat down on the low wall next to him. He took one of his headphones out.

"Hi," he said.

I smiled. I wanted to say something but didn't trust myself not to say anything completely stupid. Or my voice not to crack. I'm trying not to stare at how big his shoes are and at the same time wondering why I noticed them.

"You don't talk much, do you?" he said, smiling. "I'm Daniel."

"Aaron," I said, wanting to say more but suddenly finding my mind blank.

I could hear, though, that he was listening to U2. I recognized the song, and said the title. He smiled and leaned his head to the side. "You know the song?"

I nodded.

"I love it," he said, and sang a little of the lyric. His voice isn't fantastic, but it is sincere. He offered one headphone to me, and I took it. The sun was beginning to set, the sky going from pink to violet, and the song slowly faded out, our shoulders touching. As soon as the song was done, he tapped the back arrows and started it again. We listened to the whole thing over. The entire time, he was keeping perfect time with his fingers against his thigh. I noticed that his fingernails were cut back really far. That his watch was worn and silver and just a bit too big for his thin wrists.

When the song stopped, he took out his ear bud. I did, too. "Do you live around here?" he asked, winding the cord back up.

"Yeah. Over near the pool."

"Oh, ok. I'm on the other side, near the entrance," he said. He stood up, stepping over the low wall back onto the property. "It'll be dinner soon, so I need to head." I nodded, wanting to say more but again finding nothing in my head. "We should chat or hang out," he said. "Do you have a computer?" he asked.

"Yeah," I said. I wanted to tell him more, but for some reason I couldn't think of anything else to say.

He swiped at the screen a few times, then asked, "Or we could text or whatever. Do you have snapchat?"

"I don't have a phone," I said.

He did that thing puppies do when they hear a new sound, quirking his head to the side. "No phone?"

"Well, it's a long story. I mean, I have one...or had one...but..."

"...but you dropped it, broke the screen, and the parents said you couldn't have another one until you, and I bet I'm quoting here, 'learned to take better care of your things.'"

"Yeah," I said. Again, I wanted to say so much more, to tell him how funny he was and laugh, but instead I made a sound like a car dying.

"At least they didn't take away your computer…or did they?"

From somewhere off in the distance, we both heard someone yelling, "Daniel!"

He rolled his eyes.

"To be continued. Just come by tomorrow. I'm in 483."

Just like that it happened, as if it were the easiest thing in the world.

"Yeah," I said, standing.

"483 tomorrow?" he asked, walking away backwards.

"Yeah," I said. He smiled and turned and in a few moments was around the corner I was just hiding behind ten minutes ago.

I stood there for another five minutes at least, knowing I should go but not wanting to.

The next morning, I fidgeted around the house until my mom left for work. I'd love to be able to say I was calm, cool, and collected but that was not the case. She had the radio playing like always while she straightened out her hair.

"I'm Jim Thompson, and this is news at the top of the hour. Sad news out of Arizona, today, where a 17-year-old boy has committed suicide. The note he left said that he had always felt he was different, and that he suspected he was transgender, his parents said. This is yet another in what one researcher for the Families First group described as a wave of suicides of lesbian, gay and transgender teens over the last six years. When asked for comment, Arizona governor Bill Thorndike said, 'Any loss of a young life is tragic, but even more tragic would be a culture that condones deviant lifestyles. The true tragedy here is that there aren't more camps and facilities to help these young people find

Jesus before it's too late.' You'll remember that Thorndike was one of the major powers helping to get government assistance to centers like he describes under the Empowering Youth Act of last year. The time now is..."

"Honey, what is it?" Mom asked, her head cocked to the side and the hot iron moving through her hair.

"Huh?" I asked.

"You're pacing and fidgeting and hovering and...you just seem nervous. Is something going on?"

"No. Nope," I said.

"Okay," she said after a moment.

I went downstairs and flipped on the television. I wasn't actually paying attention to anything that was on the screen, just rotating through the channels on my favorites list. At this hour it was all news or the earliest of the morning chat shows. On one, a group of women were sitting around a table and a man in a black suit was in the middle.

"So, what is this initiative about?" one of the women asked the man.

"It's fairly simple. We think that now that good, clean, Christian prayer is a part of our children's daily lives, connecting the learning in the classroom to their spiritual needs, schools will be safer," the man said.

"That sounds wonderful," said another of the women. Many of them nodded.

"And how is it going finding support for your work?" the first woman asked.

"There has been a huge outpouring of support, Tina. People are thrilled that we are taking back our classrooms and making them safe places for Christian children to be. You know, our first initiative, the one that got so many school boards to ban things like gay and lesbian information in the curriculum, was a resounding success, and we're hoping for that same level of commitment here, too."

"Aaron?" Mom called down the steps.

"Yeah?" I called back from the couch.

"Could you take some chicken out of the freezer to thaw while I'm thinking about it?"

"Yeah," I said and went to the freezer. I pulled out a freezer bag with three chicken breasts in it and set the bag in the sink.

"God bless the work you and your group do," a woman was saying on the TV. The audience erupted in applause.

Mom came down the stairs putting an earring in. "Okay, I'm off." At the bottom of the steps she kissed my forehead then picked up her purse from the little table near the door. "You have a good day," she said, fishing her keys out from her purse and looking at me.

"What?" I asked, afraid somehow she could see through me, that she knew why I was so nervous. That somehow Daniel showed on my face.

"Nothing. You're just getting so big. Where the hell did time go?" she asked, shook her head, then left.

With her gone, I could finally stop trying to pretend I wasn't nervous, which helped. Daniel and I hadn't really set a time for me to come over, but I knew I couldn't show up at 8 in the morning. I had to stall until at least 11 or so. The idea of that much time waiting made my stomach hurt.

After thirty minutes of wandering around the house aimlessly, I finally just took some time to do what most guys do when we're alone. It was nice, and definitely took some of the edge off. After I cleared out the browser history and showered, it was finally 9:30. Once that was done, I started planning my outfit for the day. Unfortunately, it was that awful part of the wash cycle where it was not quite time to do laundry, so my favorite clothes were all dirty. I tried to decide between just making do with what I had or doing a quick load. I thought that the laundry would help pass time, so I did that.

The whole time I'm doing my best not to think about trying to talk to Daniel, to actually try to pretend I was cool enough for someone to want to hang out with me. It was all so exciting but so exhausting.

Finally, at 10:45, I was clean and had on clean shorts and my Adventure Time t-shirt. Then I was just sitting on the couch, my knees bouncing up and down, watching the clock move. On the TV, a man sat at a long table with lots of other men and women. He asked, "Jerry, here in Thompson's last full year before the election really gets heated, what does he have to do to help his party keep the White House?"

A man from down the table leaned forward, "At this point, Tom, the country has swung so decidedly conservative that I don't think the Democrats have a chance, so nothing, really. God, guns, and anti-abortion politics are here to stay."

I shut the TV off and stood up. I had one of those clear moments where the quiet of the house fell on me. My brain caught in one of those thoughts, and I realized that if something bad were to happen to me right then, there was no one around to help. I toed into my sneakers, picked up my keys from the bowl, and walked out the door, locking it behind me.

For some reason, it never even occurred to me that he might not be there. When I walked up, though, I realized I had just counted on it without knowing. The back gate was open, and he was there, sitting at a large round green plastic table on the back porch, one knee pulled up to his chest with his earphones on.

"Hi," I said.

"Hello," he said. As he brought his knee down, I tried not to look at how beautiful his leg was or how it tapered to his ankle so well. I sat down next to him. The sun was already too hot, but I didn't want to say anything that might make him move.

"So what's your last name?"

"What? Why?" I ask.

He laughs, "Is it a state secret or something?" He pushes the tip of his finger into my tummy gently, "am I not allowed to know without clearance?" I laugh and grab his hand, leaning away as if I don't want him to touch me, but keeping his finger right where it is.

"No. I mean, yeah, you can, I've just never had anybody ask me to tell them my last name, before." A bit too late, I realize that I haven't let go of his hand, yet. We're just sitting there, looking at each other, with his fingertip against my belly and my hands around his wrist keeping it there.

"So?" he says after a minute, leaning his head toward me.

"Oh!" I say, "It's Miller. Aaron Miller."

"See? Was that so hard? Do you know mine?"

"No," I say. Again, silence stretches out between us.

He rolls his eyes, "would you *like* to know mine?"

"Oh. Oh!," I say, finally letting go of his wrist. "Yeah. What's your last name?"

"It's Young."

"Daniel Young," I say.

The sun is warm on my back, and we're alone just talking, and it hits me that I am happy. Sitting here, talking about nothing, I was happy. I started to become aware, though, that the quiet had stretched on too long, and that I needed to say something.

"Why?" I ask.

"What?" he asks in return.

"The band?" I ask, wanting to shrink five times smaller and run away.

"Oh!" he says, his face softening. I've read a couple of books where someone talks about another person's smile making them feel warm all over. I always thought that had to be bullshit, but it was true. And it was happening just that fast. "Well, I like the music for one. I know they're not cool or whatever, but I like them. No one else sounds like them, you know? Especially their early stuff. I like that they are trying to change the world, too. I see people call them preachy, and get down on them for trying to do important things, but to me it's like this—other groups out there make even more money than U2 does, but what do they spend it on? Big SUVs? Parties? The guys in U2 spend their money trying to get people to help others. I mean, when was the last time Brittany Spears or Christina Aguilera tried to help people in Africa living with AIDS?" Daniel finished.

I felt so stupid and cheap and dumb. I hadn't ever tried to help anyone in Africa with AIDS. The few times Mom could afford to give me allowance, I immediately blew it on chocolate.

"My dad had this tape he'd made off of a friend's stereo. He could never bring rock music into his mom's house, he told me after I found the tape and asked him what was on it. So, he would go to a friend's house and record that guy's music and leave the tape's label blank. No writing to give it away. I found a stash of them in a box up in the attic and started to listen to them. When I got old enough, and they would let me download music," he said, wiggling his player back and forth with his thumb and forefinger, "I started to download the albums one by one. They sounded so different. Especially this one," he said, and before I could tell what he was doing, he put one of the earbuds into my ear and suddenly, yet again, we were both listening to the same music.

It curled me, though, as if I had a warm, red center, which had always been there, but I only suddenly found it. I curled around that center, the music curling with me. I couldn't even tell what instruments were being used—there was only me, my heartbeat, and a voice. I opened my eyes and Daniel was staring directly at me. I knew I should say something, I wanted to say something, but there wasn't anything to say.

He reached out and took the earbud out slowly, his forefinger grazing over the top of my ear. I'd never thought that about anyone touching my ear, before. Usually when I was thinking about someone else touching me, that was not where his hands were. In that moment, though, all I wanted was for him to keep his finger on the top of my ear.

"'With or Without You' from The Joshua Tree," he said, showing the screen on his player with the black and white cover I knew was in my stack.

"I haven't gotten to this one, yet."

"Huh?" he asked.

"Nothing," I said.

"No," he said, poking me in the tummy gently. "Say."

"Okay," I said, and took a huge breath. "I stole."

"Stole? Stole what?"

I gestured toward his player. "From the library. I copied the disks to my hard drive."

He started laughing. I didn't know if I should feel insulted or not.

"That's not stealing," he said when he finally stopped laughing.

"It is, though," I said.

"Well, yeah; I mean, technically it is. But it isn't. And trust me, I don't think they'd mind all that much. I think Bono would rather you had the music, and that it hopefully inspires you to do something important. I mean, if you had paid, they could use that money for fuel for the jet to get to Washington to get some congressman to agree to vote for a bill to help someone, somewhere, but trust me—I think he'd rather you have the music."

"Do you think so?"

He nodded, and I felt a bit better.

I heard a huge vehicle pull up somewhere close. "Shit," he said, leaning forward. "My mom, back from the grocery store. I'll have to help get everything settled and then it'll be lunchtime for the troops. That's what my mom calls all of us. Then naptime which I have to help with. Maybe...maybe back here tomorrow?" he asked.

Everything was happening so fast.

"Sure," I said.

He stood up and turned away, then turned back. "I'm on YouTube."

"What?" I asked.

"If you wanted to look up my videos or whatever. I'm on YouTube. If you want."

I nodded. "How do I...?"

He pulled a pen out of his pocket with one hand and grabbed my wrist with the other. With just a bit of pressure, he brought my palm up and on it wrote a series of letters and numbers. "That's me," he said. "Also, this," he said, writing another word just below it. "That's me on Yahoo chat," he said, rolling his eyes a little. "I know, it's very 2002, but it's freeware, so..."

"Oh," I said, then realized what he was saying, what he was giving me, "Oh!" Then I realized his hand was touching me. I wanted to close my eyes and just feel it, but it was over before I could stop myself.

"Yeah. So, like, you can go watch them if you want."

I honestly don't remember what I said or what the walk home was like. I only remember feeling invincible and lighter than air just like all the stupid songs say.

VIKTOR

I knew from the first moment that he said that name. Don't ask me how. It just happens to me sometimes that I can see where the train is going long before it pulls into the station.

"Have you seen the other one around? The Aaron kid?" Marcus asked.

Sinking feeling.

"I have. He and the target seem to be getting closer."

"Yes," Marcus said. And just like that, I knew. But I didn't want to, so I ignored it.

And now look at where we are.

AARON

I went all the way back and watched every single one of his videos. They started out goofy, with bad lighting, Daniel just rambling on, full of "um" and "uh." But over time, as his haircut changed, and his face grew into the one I recognized, the pauses came out, and he began to speak fluidly. The subjects went from movie reviews to his thoughts on books that they read in school to books he was reading on his own to his thoughts on politics.

"Hey," Mom said from the doorway. I looked up and saw from the light in the room that it was late in the day. I must've been playing them for hours. "You going to go outside sometime today?" Sometime over the summer, she'd become concerned that I wasn't getting outside enough. What was out there that she considered so important for me to somehow get through osmosis, I had no idea.

"No," I joked.

She frowned and ducked out the door. The next video was the one he made the night Thompson was elected the first time. I clicked on it. He was sitting in his chair near a desk as he had been in several videos before, but the light that usually framed his face wasn't on. It was hard to see him as more than a blur in the background.

"So, obviously, I'm pretty disappointed. Right now, across the country, people full of hate are celebrating themselves. Celebrating the victory of their values over the hope of change. They think that *Leave it to Beaver* was a documentary, and that somehow, they can bring that version of the 50s back. I can't help but feel that all of what Mr. Dalton, my English teacher, calls 'the talking heads' are right—that if more young people would just get out and vote, this could have been avoided. But just like he says, we're convinced we don't have any real say. Everyone in 9th grade civics hears about the electoral college and takes it the wrong way. Everyone learns for the first time about the military industrial complex and thinks they don't have a chance. Things like tonight, with the people who not only don't want change, but to roll the clock backward...it's things like this that convince people there's no use." Then he shut off the camera.

Of course, I vaguely remember how fast things went downhill for gay people after that election. It was never the President's direct wish that laws were put in place to permanently bar gay couples from adopting, or that some states went so far as to demand that all teachers at public schools had to disclose their sexual orientation, but those things happened, and he didn't do anything to stop them.

"It's like..." Daniel said in a video from a few months after the election, "it's like these people have been encouraged to do all the terrible things they've always wanted to do now that they know no one is going to stop them." Watching his videos made me feel ashamed because I'd never been all that interested in politics. He was the same age and already had opinions on things. He already understood what the struggle was like.

Not long after that, only about a year before the day we'd met, he made a coming out video. I cried all the way through it as he dialed his mom and then told her right there on camera. She cried, too, but said so many loving, amazing things. I couldn't help but look toward my own empty bedroom doorway more than once. Not that my mother wouldn't have said loving things had I ever come out to her. She and I, we just didn't have that kind of relationship. There had never been any long heart-to-heart talks on the couch. Later in his video, Daniel sat down with his dad at a long table in what must have been their kitchen at the time. When he said, "Dad, I'm gay," I had to pause the video I was crying so hard. When I finally got control of myself again, I tapped play again. His father didn't say anything, just immediately swept Daniel up into a standing hug, and I was open-mouthed sobbing. The video wound out to its end with them just holding one another. I had to close my laptop and push it off my chest. I curled into a ball and cried.

After that the videos were still about how horrible things were happening legally and how suicides were in the news every day, but Daniel himself seemed lighter. It wasn't as if he was happy about anything he was talking about, but he did seem to be less disturbed. I kept dreading that there would be some kind of boyfriend video, but there wasn't. Either he hadn't had one, or he hadn't put any details in a video. Eventually, almost the next to last video was about moving. He talked about how scared he was, how much crap he was throwing away, and about his hopes that he might finally find someone to kiss. I smiled a bit. The next video was from on the road. They'd stayed at a crappy motel and he made a video down by the pool. I felt more than a little pervy, but I liked looking at his shoulders under the straps of his tank top. I liked the way his collarbones were almost straight across instead of angled like mine. The last video was from the inside of an apartment that looked a lot like mine, and was the day of the move-in. He gave a quick tour and then had an argument on camera with one of his brothers about who would get what bedroom. Daniel's parents had promised him that he might finally have a room of his own, but one of his brothers wanted to stay in that room, too. It was fun to watch him be a little petty and normal. Eventually his mom stepped in and Daniel got the room to himself. When he finished panning around, I noticed with a shock that he'd chosen the exact same bedroom as I had, though their townhouse had several more bedrooms than the one my mom and I shared. We were both in the back overlooking the back patio and parking lot beyond.

7:48 pm

Idontknowwhattoputhere12: Hello
In_The_Shadows_42: Hello who's this?
Idontknowwhattoputhere12: It's me
In_The_Shadows_42: This better not be Hunter because I told you
Idontknowwhattoputhere12: No, it's me, Aaron
In_The_Shadows_42: to stay away
In_The_Shadows_42: Oh!
In_The_Shadows_42: Hi!
Idontknowwhattoputhere12: Hi. Who's Hunter?
In_The_Shadows_42: It is a very very long story that I promise I will share some other time.
In_The_Shadows_42: You made it on. That's great. How did you get past the mobile phone number requirement?
Idontknowwhattoputhere12: I do have a number, remember, just not a phone.
In_The_Shadows_42: Oh, yeah. Okay.
Idontknowwhattoputhere12: So. I watched your videos.
In_The_Shadows_42: Stalker ;)
In_The_Shadows_42: And?
Idontknowwhattoputhere12: I like your old haircut better ;)
In_The_Shadows_42: Bastard! Did you like them?

Idontknowwhattoputhere12: It's funny I watch some gay vloggers but mostly not. I hadn't seen yours, though.
In_The_Shadows_42: I will try not to be offended by that.
Idontknowwhattoputhere12: No, I mean, I wish I had.
In_The_Shadows_42: Why don't you watch other gay YouTubers?
Idontknowwhattoputhere12: I don't want to say
In_The_Shadows_42: Why?
Idontknowwhattoputhere12: It's stupid
In_The_Shadows_42: Why is it stupid?
Idontknowwhattoputhere12: They make me feel dumb and lazy and I don't know
In_The_Shadows_42: How do they do that?
Idontknowwhattoputhere12: Nevermind
In_The_Shadows_42: Did my stuff make you feel that way?
Idontknowwhattoputhere12: Maybe a little
In_The_Shadows_42: I'm sorry, then.
In_The_Shadows_42: I just got the 5 minute warning.
Idontknowwhattoputhere12: The what?
In_The_Shadows_42: 5 more minutes until I have to log off.
Idontknowwhattoputhere12: Like a curfew?
In_The_Shadows_42: Yeah.
Idontknowwhattoputhere12: How old are you?
In_The_Shadows_42: A lady never tells, and a gentleman wouldn't ask ;)
In_The_Shadows_42: 17. But it wouldn't matter. I think I could be 27 and they'd still

come to my house
and make me log off and come be with the
family or read
or do anything else but what I want.
Idontknowwhattoputhere12: Ok.
In_The_Shadows_42: Come over tomorrow.
Idontknowwhattoputhere12: Ok.
In_The_Shadows_42: I have to go; the warden has arrived. Goodnight.
Idontknowwhattoputhere12: Goodnight.

When I went by his place, the back gate was closed. When I peeked over the top of the fence, he wasn't there. Something told me I'd find him at our low wall, though. I walked that way and stopped for a second when I saw him sitting there by himself. That was when it hit me on a conscious level: I wanted to touch his hair, put my hand on the small of his back, to kiss him—the word gay meant me.

I am gay, I said to myself, in my head, afraid to let it touch my lips.

I am a gay person.

He happened to turn at that moment and waved me over.

"Okay," I said, sitting down on the low wall next to him.

"Okay?" he asked. "Careful, the brick is really hot."

I tugged my shorts to make sure no part of my skin touched the wall. He had a bag of popcorn and offered me some. We snacked on popcorn for a while, and I bounced my heels off of the wall for a while.

"So, seriously, though; did you like my videos?"

"I did," I say.

"The election night one was rough," he said after a while. "I took it down not long after posting it. Which sucked because I worked a long time on getting it edited but it just never worked right."

"Why?"

"Why did it not work right?" he asked.

"No, why did you take it down?"

"Oh. It was too depressing. I made a decision that even if I was depressed, and I was, there is such a thing as too sad for a video. I've seen lots of videos out there where the person is borderline suicidal, and it causes their viewers to get really upset. I thought, what if there's some kid out there who is watching who doesn't have as good a support network as I do, and I put this video up saying that I felt there wasn't much hope and then that kid kills him or herself? That would be on me. So, instead, I decided it was better to just say nothing."

"But it was up," I said.

"It took me a long time to get it how I wanted it, but eventually I did. I put it back up just recently. I mean, it didn't make any difference then, but who knows. Maybe someone will see it in the future and it'll get them thinking about things," he said.

I don't know what made me brave enough, but without thinking about it, I slid my hand into his hand. It was only the second after I did it that I worried he might not be okay with that. To my relief, he took my hand, wove his fingers in with mine, and squeezed. We sat there like that for a long time and he hummed.

We started meeting at the low wall at the edge of the complex every day. Sometimes we'd just hold hands and stare out at the empty lot and the highway far beyond it, shimmering in the heat. Sometimes we'd talk about his videos and what he hoped to do with them. Sometimes we'd talk about the terrible things that people said about gay people on the news every day. Sometimes we'd share headphones and listen to U2 together. We'd spend time there, then go home for dinner, then chat for a while until his parents made him log off. My mom never did.

Those days, looking back, were a kind of utopia. We could have gone to my apartment, or to his family's place, but we chose to stay there, even in the heat, because there we didn't have to be who we were to anyone else—we could be who we were to each other. A place away from all other places where we could simply be us. The world outside raged that gay people were abominations, that we'd face the wrath of God if we acted on our sick, twisted impulses, but in our little bubble, our wall at the edge of the empire, the only voice besides ours was an Irish singer and his friends, weary, but still hoping for better.

Over those few days, I came to know Daniel's smell and his sounds. The things that identify a person but aren't words. He preferred the kinds of socks that don't show over shoes. He liked gray or black shorts. He smelled clean even though we were both sweating in the sun. When he wasn't paying attention, he would move his right foot along with the beat, but always just a bit off. He would tilt his head just a bit to the right whenever he didn't quite understand something, like a puppy hearing a new sound.

I started to feel something I'd never felt before during those days, too. It wasn't lust; being a teenage boy, I was already very aware of what that felt like. It was like that, but deeper, as if the two things were different shades of the same color. One was dark and lovely, but the other deeper, more beautiful because of its mystery. When he wasn't around, I wanted him to be. Even when he was there next to me, his elbow touching my thigh or some other small way that people connect, I felt like he wasn't close enough. When he smiled at me, I never wanted that smile to stop.

When we finally had to separate and go home, I would immediately close myself in my room, turn the lights off, and listen to all the same songs we'd listened to that day again and I would wait for the little dot next to his screen name to go from gray to green. I would close my eyes and try to summon him by my side, to feel his knee pressed against my ankle, or his fingers tapping the drum beat out on my thigh. Sometimes we wouldn't say anything at all. He would ask me what song I had on, then he'd put the same one on and we would just watch the cursor blink.

"We could Skype," he typed.

"No camera," I said.

"Where did your dad go to get a laptop with no camera in it, the 1950s?"

In the morning, I would put on his videos as I cleaned the house or got dressed so that I could always hear his voice.

"You're awfully quiet the last week or so," Mom said at dinner one night.

"Hmm?" I said, coming out of thinking about how great it would be if he were here at the table with me.

"I said you're awfully quiet. Your door is always closed. You don't watch TV with me anymore. What's going on?" Mom asked. "Is it already that time?" she asked. Knowing her, thinking back on it, it must've taken enormous courage to broach the subject this directly. It wasn't her style. If I'd been paying attention at the time, I would have seen that. I wasn't, though.

"What time?" I asked.

"Time for you to become a mopey teenager. The snarling, shuffling beast that all the parenting guides warned me about?" she asked with a smirk.

"Nothing's going on, mom," I said, just wanting to get back to the space in my head where Daniel was here beside me at the table.

"Are you sure? You know you can talk to me about anything, right?"

"Mom," I said.

"Okay," she said, palms up as if to surrender.

I drifted back to my own world and she sat eating alone.

I had just decided that I was going to invite Daniel back to my apartment again where, I'll be honest, I hoped something more intimate than music would happen, when someone said, "Hello."

We both turned around to find the man I'd seen at the soda machines a few weeks back, the Tai Chi guy, as I thought of him at that time.

"Hi," Daniel said.

"I see you two out here every day staring off in that direction," he said, pointing, "and I finally got curious as to what it was that was over here."

"Oh," Daniel said.

"Marcus," he said, stepping closer.

"Daniel," Daniel said, then nodded his head toward me, "Aaron."

"Hello," Marcus said, stepping even closer. Even now, thinking back on this, I'm screaming at myself to run, to hit him, to yell for help, to do *something* other than what I do next.

"Hello," I said and smiled, "Do you live here?" I asked.

"Yeah," he said, "In fact, we ran into each other awhile ago," he said, smiling at me.

"Yeah," Daniel said, "I've seen you around."

Daniel and I hadn't had any conversation about what we were at that point. There had been quite a bit of physical attention, and a lot of hand holding, but there wasn't any name to it.

Marcus stepped over the low wall and then sat down. He asked what the name of the highway was, and I told him. I'm guessing he already knew, but you see, this was part of the seduction. The shape of his body hadn't escaped my notice, nor Daniel's I'm assuming. With each gesture, we saw the cut of each muscle, the straightness of each bone. It was no accident.

"I just moved here from back east," Marcus said.

"I just moved here, too," Daniel said.

"You two are the first people I've talked to in days. Besides the movers, I mean. People around here don't seem very friendly."

"It's a very conservative town," I said because I'd heard my mother say it before. Marcus nodded.

"What is there to do around here?" Marcus asked.

"Not a lot, I think," Daniel said, looking at me.

I named a few things that I knew were tourist attractions from commercials. I thought, even as I was saying them, though, that I'd never been to any of those places. Marcus nodded along.

"That hiking trail sounds interesting," he said. "Have you been?"

"No," I said. Daniel shook his head as well.

"Oh," Marcus said, "then—no, nevermind."

"What?" Daniel asked.

"Nothing. I was just all caught up in the moment. Forget it."

"No—say," Daniel prodded.

"Well, I was just going to say that if none of us have gone, then we should all go together, but then I realized how creepy that would sound from someone whom you just met five seconds ago, so I stopped myself."

"Ah," Daniel said. As if scripted, we all turned our attention to the highway in the distance once more. "I mean, I guess it could sound all creepy, but that wouldn't be fair of us." Daniel must've seen the expression on my face because he went on, "I mean, people are always complaining about how harsh the world can be, how mean people are, but then we have all these rules that say we can't talk to this person or that person. We put up all these little walls or whatever. I wonder what would happen if people were more open when they met."

Marcus smiled and the light caught his eyes just right. I found myself smiling back at him.

"So, what if, just what if, we all decided to make friends even though we only met you five minutes ago?" Daniel asked.

"I think it'd be really cool, but I'm a bit biased," Marcus said. They both turned to look at me.

"You're not—I mean, you're not some killer or some Jesus freak, are you?" I asked.

Marcus' face got very still in that way he had, and he said, "The homosexual is an abomination to our world and must be eradicated," and chills went across my shoulders. For those two seconds, the coldness and fury in his eyes was overpowering, like staring down a snake. Then he smiled and snorted and we all laughed. "No, I am not a 'Jesus freak,'" he said. "I tell you what—if it's agreed that instead of just making small talk and then moving on with our separate lives we're actually going to connect as two new people and a native of this great city, what about dinner? My treat? Pizza?"

"Sure," Daniel said. That's his open heart, you see. That was his magic.

"Great," Marcus said, "maybe pizza tomorrow night?" Then he smiled this crooked smile that made his whole face change.

And even now, hearing Daniel say "okay" again, as I know he will, as I know he must, I'm still screaming at my younger self to stop this, to run away, to remember everything he'd ever been told about strangers and the danger they pose, anything to try to change how this whole thing turns out. But Daniel says "okay" the same way he did then, and

Marcus smiles and says, "great."

And the whole thing is set in motion.

"Come in," Marcus said and closed the door behind us. I'd immediately noticed there wasn't a TV or the giant rack of DVDs next to it that most people I knew seemed to have. I was trying not to think about how grown it made me feel to be standing in an adult's apartment without another adult around. Daniel was playing it off, but I got the feeling he felt the same.

"You don't own a TV?" I asked and hated myself as soon as it was out of my stupid mouth. Daniel and I had both told our parents that we were having dinner at the other's house and then walked directly to the apartment number Marcus had given us. As soon as he'd opened the door, we had both stood there for a moment staring at his immaculate space. There weren't many decorations, but everything seemed to be in the perfect place, including his set of Japanese swords on the far wall.

"No," Marcus said, "movies and TV rot your brain. I read books, instead. Here," he said, walking past us to the table and then hands us both mugs of tea, though they don't have the fruity smell of anything that my mom has in the house. He walked us down a short hallway to a room. He flicked on the light, and on all four walls are bookshelves, the ones you get from a store and put together. I know because we have several, only there are no books on them, just pictures and scrapbooks.

"Have you read all of these?" Daniel asked, walking to the nearest case.

He laughed. "Everyone asks that. Is it so unusual to read?"

I don't say anything, but instead touch the spines. I wanted to be able to talk about them with him, but don't know any of the titles.

"I'll be right back," Marcus said to me. While he was in the bathroom, I read over the spines of the books. They were all by authors I'd never heard of: Ian Fleming, John Le Carré, Robert Ludlum, John Gardner. All were paperbacks, and most of them were deeply creased, bowing inward. On the next shelf down, the books were all by Samuel R. Delany. Next to those were books by Dennis Cooper and Bret Easton Ellis.

"Wow," I said, looking at Daniel.

"I know," he mouthed to me.

"Do you know any of them?" Marcus asked from behind me. I jumped, because I didn't hear him come back.

"No," I said. "I want to read more, but I..." for some reason, I can't figure out how to finish that sentence.

"Are these all yours?" Daniel asked.

"Not all, no. Most of them were already here. This isn't my place, really," Marcus said.

"Whose is it?" Daniel asked.

Marcus steps forward and puts his hand on a row of books, "It's okay, you know. I didn't like reading much, either, until someone explained it to me." A chill ran down my back as I realized that I wanted his hand on me like that. "Someone told me that the brain is a muscle. You have to work it every day the same way that you work an arm or a leg. If you want a stronger brain, you have to work it every day," he said, and I can tell that in his head, he just heard the voice of the person who told him that. He looked at me, "at the time, I was working very hard on my body, but I wasn't getting any smarter. So I made it a point to read every day. Like doing crunches for your mind," he said, smirking. "Do you know where Free Verse is?"

I shook my head.

"I didn't, either, when I first moved here. I'll show you. It's the only bookstore in town owned by a gay man. All the employees are gay homeless kids. Anyway, the guy who owns it, Tim, he showed me what was the good stuff and what was the bad stuff. At first, I just had to trust him, but after a while, I could see it myself. He started me off with Delany," Marcus says, again running his hand over a novel called *The Stars in my Pockets like Grains of Sand* as if it were someone's thigh. "Then he showed me transgressive stuff," he said, putting his fingertips on a novel called *Try*, then moving it over to one called *Less Than Zero*. "When I told Tim about what I wanted to be, the way I wanted to be, he showed me how to tell the good stuff from the bad stuff in what he called 'genre fiction,'" he said, putting his hand on a novel called *Tinker, Tailor, Soldier, Spy*.

"I should read more," I said, and found myself surprised at how much I meant it.

"Me, too," Daniel said.

Marcus looked at a nearby shelf, blinks once, moves to the shelf below it, then pulls a particular book. The book he hands Daniel has the title *The Stars in My Pockets*... "Here," he said.

"Oh, um, I..." Daniel started, trying to think of a way to give it back to him.

"Stop," he said, "breathe. It's okay to take things from someone if they offer it to you. Take it. Read it. Or don't read it. But I'm giving it to you."

"Okay. I'll try to get it back to you..."

"Stop," he said, "breathe." And what's odd is that I had stopped breathing for a second. "I don't lend books; I'm giving this to you. It's yours. What you have to decide is are you Marq or are you Rat."

"I don't..." Daniel started.

"You'll understand when you're done reading it," he said, and moves from the bookshelf to the kitchen. I follow. "Pizza should be here soon," he said over his shoulder.

When we get to the kitchen, he sat down against the far wall. Daniel and I sat on the opposite side. When he's sitting down, Marcus' sleeves pull back a bit, and I can see the outlines of his arms. They are powerful, the veins right near the surface. He catches me looking. "I work out a lot," he said. He picked up his own mug of tea and sips.

"I can tell," I said. His left eyebrow shot up. I realized that what he just heard must have sounded like a pickup line from a stupid movie. "Oh, no, I just meant that..." I started to say but realized I don't know how to finish that sentence.

"So," he said, "how long have you two been together?"

I choked a bit, and accidentally put the mug down too hard. "What?" I sputter.

He smiled, "You're both gay. It's okay, there's nothing to worry about—I'm gay, too."

"I," I start, but stall. Realizing I hadn't finished a sentence, I said, "I know." Then I realize that he might get offended by me saying that, as though he were too obvious or something, and I started to say something else, but he put a hand up.

"Relax. Breathe. It's okay—I don't want to hide from them," he said, motioning toward the large window nearby with his head. "I don't want to hide, so I don't try to. If they have a problem with who I am, then it's their problem."

"We're...kind of new," Daniel said. Marcus nodded as if he was expecting that exact sentence. I smiled at Daniel.

"But...aren't you afraid, sometimes?" I asked.

"I used to be, when I was your age," he said, looking down at the table, then back at me, "all the time. But not now."

"Why not now?" I asked.

"I've learned to take care of myself. Of the people I care about," he said and the doorbell rang. Marcus went to answer it.

"I want to bring over the camera sometime," Daniel said, "interview this guy for one of my videos."

"He's really cool," I said. Daniel nodded.

Marcus comes back and puts the pizza on the table. "Here we are," he said.

Marcus put a wine glass in front of me. The wine was so dark I couldn't see through it, unlike the pinkish stuff my mom bought for herself every once in a while. It all felt edgy and dangerous all of a sudden. A part of me wanted to say what I'd been programmed to say since first grade, "I don't drink alcohol." The truth was, though, that I didn't know if I did or not. And sitting in Marcus' house made me feel independent, separate from what I was. I liked that Marcus hadn't even asked Daniel and I, but merely fixed us glasses as if we were just like him.

"Cheeky little red," he said, and for the first time I heard a bit of an accent. Daniel sipped from his glass and made a bit of a face but tried to cover it. I pulled a slice onto one of the plates that Marcus had also put on the table while I'd been watching Daniel. As Daniel pulled his slice and Marcus sat down, I took a sip of my own. I wish I could say that I liked it, and then name off all the tastes and ingredients like someone on one of those cooking shows, but all I tasted was bitter.

If Marcus noticed either of our reactions, he didn't make it apparent.

The pizza was greasy and had too much sauce and was amazing. I kept reminding myself to eat slower than I normally would have because I was in front of company, but it was hard. I found after a few sips the wine tasted better, too.

"So, what do you two do when you're not sitting on walls wanting to hold hands?" Marcus asked grinning.

Daniel laughed, then put his hand up in front of his mouth, "I have a YouTube channel."

"Do you?" Marcus asked. Daniel nodded and looked at me.

"I don't really do anything," I said.

"What sort of videos do you make?" Marcus asked Daniel.

"Stuff about being gay. Statistics of suicide rates, stories about abuse, I did a few about the reparation therapy camps, stuff like that."

"Interesting," Marcus said, then took a drink from his wine. "Have you done one, then, about how gay themes are all over the place in what people think of as 'straight' literature?"

Daniel shook his head no, but was chewing again, so he gestured for Marcus to go on.

"So, take, for instance, Fagin and Dodger," he said, and looked over at the wall. I could tell he was looking at his bookshelves, even though they were back in the other room. He knew exactly where they were, even though he couldn't see them. "From *Oliver Twist*. The clever thief street boys and the kindly old queer who runs them. Dickens knew what things were like. He had to keep the details out, or the book wouldn't sell, but people were much smarter back then, anyway. Most of them understood what he was getting at."

"What was he...?" I started to ask, but stopped myself. I remembered the second I started talking that I hadn't really read the book. I'd heard people talk about it, and seen a stupid movie they made because my English teacher thought that seeing the movie was the same as reading the book, but I'd never read it.

"Why would the old man, Fagin, be kind to a pack of street boys? Dickens shows that he could just as well have beat them and still gotten whatever they'd stolen off of them to support himself. Instead, though, he's kind. He loves them. When Philip is arrested and taken from the group, Fagin is heartbroken. It serves Dodger, though. Dodger, who was Fagin's head boy. The one he really loved all along."

I looked over at Daniel. His eyes were locked on Marcus'.

"He was right, too, you know. About groups of street boys. About their handlers. There are the good ones, and the bad ones. Millions of little armies all over the world. I wonder if there were other groups operating at the same time as Fagin's group," his eyes focused again, and it was almost like I was looking at someone different. A chill ran down my back. "When I think about that book, I wonder, sometimes. If Fagin or Dodger had thought to combine the other groups of boys around the city, what could they have been able to accomplish?"

"I don't remember any of those parts," I said.

"Me, either, but I can totally see it," Daniel said, his voice almost a whisper.

A smile touched the corners of his lips, but then was gone, "Most people don't. We get too caught up in Philip's story to think about Dodger." He sipped from his wine again, and for a moment we were all quiet, eating. "Sorry," he said after a while, "I like to read."

"I should read more," I said. I found that, at that moment, the thing I wanted most was for him to respect me.

"You should," he said. Later, I would think about that moment, and those words could have been an insult. I didn't feel like they were, though. In that moment it felt like he was holding open a door for me.

"What should I start with?" I asked.

"I can't tell you that. That's what one of my dearest friends said to me. Your path through the wilderness of narratives, he said to me, is your own. Each book is a step in a journey toward who you are, who you're going to be. You have to take those steps alone," for some reason, as he said this, the room seemed to get quieter, like that moment just after the air conditioner has shut off after running for so long you'd forgotten it.

Daniel hadn't said anything in a while, so I looked at him. He was just staring at Marcus.

"What do you like to read?" I asked.

"A lot of things. Things that help me see between the lines." He gestured to the stack I'd flipped through. "Like those you were looking at. Ways to see what's going on in fiction. How they program us using the stories they tell. Books that help me 'resist the dominant narratives,'" he said, and I could tell that last part was quoting someone, because his voice changed.

"Like what?" I asked.

"Comic books," he said, and sipped.

I couldn't help but laugh, but stopped immediately when I could see how serious he was. "Aren't," Daniel smiled at me, "aren't those for, like, little kids?"

"They were, at one time. Now the superhero comics are a place where writers work through our ideas about power, social responsibility, and the nature of morality." I could tell by his tone, he thought this was all completely obvious. "Do you know who Northstar is?" he asked.

"No," I said.

"He's the first openly gay comic book character. Marvel comics, Alpha Flight, volume 1, issue 106. There had probably been other characters that the writers intended to be gay at other companies, but there were policies in place that kept them from saying it outright. Scott Lobdell was the writer of Alpha Flight at the time, though, and he got permission to have the character announce it at a press conference in the issue."

I didn't know what to say, so I nodded.

"Here's the problem. Every time a new writer came around, they killed Northstar off. Every time. He died in some pretty horrible ways, sometimes even offstage. It was like we had won this tiny little victory... an openly gay superhero...that's not that much to ask..." he trailed off, then took a sip of wine. As he did, I looked at my own glass and found I'd somehow drunk half of it. "But then every other writer who comes along has to assert how much better straights are by killing him off." Marcus leaned back in his chair. "If you look at gay characters in literature, comic books, movies, any of it, there is nothing they like more than to kill us off."

"I'd really like to record you for one of my videos," Daniel said.

"No," Marcus said, taking another sip.

"Why?" Daniel asked.

"I don't like to be photographed or recorded."

"But you have some great things to say that I think need to be heard, especially by other kids like me who are out there."

I watched something play over Marcus' face at that point, but then he shook his head and said, "no," with a finality that clearly meant the conversation was over.

We ate a bit more in silence, chatted a bit more, but two things became clear by the time Daniel and I left twenty minutes later. One was that Marcus was much more interested in Daniel as a person than he was me, and the second was that something about Marcus wasn't ordinary. He wasn't just some person. The third thing became clear only in retrospect, and that was that I was starting to become infatuated with Marcus.

7:51 pm

Idontknowwhattoputhere12: What do you think of this Marcus guy?

In_The_Shadows_42: He's really passionate. A little scary. You?

Idontknowwhattoputhere12: Same.

In_The_Shadows_42: I was thinking I might have him on a video

Idontknowwhattoputhere12: He seemed to know a lot about gay things. History and stuff.

In_The_Shadows_42: Yeah. There's the five minute warning. See you tomorrow?

Idontknowwhattoputhere12: Yeah. Why don't you come over here?

In_The_Shadows_42: Ok. Goodnight.

Idontknowwhattoputhere12: Goodnight.

MARCUS

File 2618-69370-B

Index: 8-07:41

Room 1159B

Transcript follows:

Harper: Good morning.

Prisoner: (makes a noise)

Harper: (papers shuffling) I'd like to revisit some of the basic facts of the whole thing. Ask some questions about them.

Prisoner: As if I had any choice.

Harper: So you picked this kid, Daniel Young, because he had this YouTube channel, correct? That he had a visible presence and people would take more notice of him if he were the bomber than perhaps others.

Prisoner: We've been over this already

Harper: As I said, I want to go over it again. All of that was correct, yes?

Prisoner: Yes

Harper: Okay. Okay. Here's where I'm getting caught up, though he was a child. I get that you want someone with a visible presence, someone who is gay and would start out already somewhat sympathetic to your cause. I get that. But why a child?

Prisoner: This is the problem with your system, with the way you people think.

Harper: What is?

Prisoner: When someone is from a suppressed class, they grow up earlier. A straight sixteen-year-old boy is still somewhat a child, though even that is reductive. But a gay boy at seventeen has already become aware that the world hates him. How long could you stay a child, if the definition of childhood is innocence, which you all define as a lack of experience, if you knew, knew, that the world you lived in hated you.

Harper: Hated is a bit of a strong word, don't you think?

Prisoner: That's how far out of reality you are. All the investigative might of the FBI behind you, and you still know fuck all. You should be embarrassed.

Harper: I should be embarrassed? Might I remind you, you're the one who seduced a child and then convinced that child to blow himself up for your cause.

Prisoner: He's a saint. He will forever be remembered by us.

Harper: I'm sure that's a real fucking comfort to him from the grave. You knowingly got close to a sixteen-year-old boy with the intent of having sex with him and then used your sexual relationship to convince him to become a suicide bomber for your organization. You ask me? That's pretty fucking despicable, pal.

Prisoner: That shows how little you understand. He's a hero, now. You're just a tool of your government.

Harper: Be that as it may, tell me why the switch? Why did you switch from wanting Daniel Young to Aaron Miller? It seems to me that was a fairly big deviation from your plan.

Prisoner: I'm guessing that at no point will this case go to trial.

Harper: Not that it has anything to do with what I'm asking, but yeah I'm guessing when we're done with you here, it'll be air convict for you until we find someone willing to take you in and disappear you for us. Who knows how long that'll take. Why do you ask?

Prisoner: "Justice for all."

Harper: Don't give me that shit. Do you think, if we ever were to put you on the stand, you'd get anything approaching justice the way you want it? Just for having sex with an underage boy any jury alive would destroy the rest of your life. Add to that convincing him to blow himself up and a fucking church that was in the middle of a wedding to boot? You're a child molester and a child murderer, pal. You'd be on a table with lethal chemicals pumped through you so fast it'd make your head spin. But don't tell me, let me guess you were hoping to use your time on the stand to try to make your point to the world? Now who's the naïve one?

Prisoner: Underage boy. Are you listening to yourself? Your laws, your deranged overactive puritanical culture put them both on the front lines just as your culture's lack of intervention put me on mine, put Viktor on his. There are no such things as children in a warzone, Agent Harper.

Harper: This isn't a warzone. This is the suburbs. This isn't Syria or Pakistan.

Prisoner: Is it not? Truly?

Harper: You can't expect that anyone will take you

seriously if you're arguing that somehow two teenage boys, two children, sitting in their bedrooms, took up arms to defend themselves against an invading force. That's ludicrous.

Prisoner: Aaron is a hero of the cause. His name will forever be remembered. Your straight culture, your Christ culture forced him to have to defend himself every day. Of course, you'd have preferred that he stay unarmed, that he somehow not know he had power to disrupt. Naturally you would all rather I not have told him anything he needed to know. It is for that very reason that I did it.

Harper: So you admit to the crime of inciting radicalized behavior in a teenage boy, that you seduced him into your terrorist cell and that you always had the intent to give him access to explosives and weapons?

Prisoner: I admit to freeing a young person from the tyranny of over-Christianized, mandatory-heterosexuality rape culture and to giving him a place, a place that your Westernized bullshit culture couldn't.

Harper: We're done here.

AARON

On Daniel's second visit to my house, we were up in my room. The first visit had made me so nervous that we didn't stay long before I'd ushered us out and back to our spot on the low wall. I just kept seeing mom come home early for something and find us there and think we were...you know. Which I wish we would be, but I didn't want her to think we were.

It's complicated.

This time, though, I made myself not freak out. I forced myself to breathe. "So, I've been wondering something," Daniel said, leaning back onto his elbow on my bed. I was sitting in the chair at my desk, desperately trying not to look at how nice his legs tapered to his ankles. I tried not to think about how close his head was to where I slept.

We'd spent some time downstairs watching the cartoon network, then he'd asked to see my room, which he hadn't gotten to see during the first visit. Before I could really say yes or no, he was already upstairs. I worried that I might have left my laptop open and that there might be some pictures up that I wouldn't want him to see. Luckily enough, the computer was closed, and he flopped onto my bed. We'd been chatting about my poster of Daniel Craig and about Bond movies, when he asked.

"Yeah?"

"There's...there's kind of this thing in a few weeks that I'd like to go to, but I don't want to go alone. In fact, I don't think my parents would let me go alone," he said.

Quiet stretched out again. Then he said, "there's this guy, kind of like an important guy in the LGBTQ community. I want to make a whole video about it."

"What's that?"

"What, LGBTQ?"

"Yeah,"

"It stands for lesbian, gay, bisexual, transgender, and the q stands for both queer and questioning. There are supposed to be other letters, too, but I can never get them in the right order. Which is bad, because they're important, but it's hard to remember them all."

"What's...what's questioning?"

"Well, I mean, remember—I have had to read about all this stuff. It's not like I'm some expert or anything. From what the forums say, it means both people who spend a lot of time questioning their sexuality, as in not knowing definitively if they're one of the other letters, and it also means people who question the need to have all the labels and categories," he said.

"Oh," I said, feeling confused and like I understood all at the same time.

"So, this guy is coming, and he's kind of, I dunno, a leader in the community. Winston Mendez—have you heard of him? An important guy. I really want to hear him speak, but from what I can see, the hall he's going to speak in is way downtown. If we were back in Portland, my parents would let me go, but here..."

"Sure," I said, "I'll go."

His face lit up, "Really?"

"Yeah," I said, and he put his hand on my shoulder and squeezed. He took it away again almost immediately, but I wanted it to stay.

"Awesome! You won't have to pay for gas or anything. I'll take care of it. It's going to be so cool." His watch beeped. We both looked at it. "Gotta jet. The parents aren't too hover-y, but they do appreciate a punctual teenager."

"Okay; see you tomorrow?"

"Yeah," he said as if it meant 'of course, and you're silly to even ask.'

VIKTOR

I never say, "I told you so." Predicting the future is boring. So is revenge. The only thing that matters, that has ever mattered, is the now. I learned this early growing up in Al-Tall. If you stay in the now, you don't hurt or cry or go hungry.

The now is here with Ji Yoen curled against me on one side and Abeo on the other. My mind starts to think that we shouldn't be trying to bring a child into this war. My mind starts to wonder what we've become when we consider using a boy this young to make our point. Are we shirking our own duty? Why not one of us, those of us who committed to this long ago?

Abeo pushes his pelvis into mine. It helps me to get out of my head and back into the now. Across the room I can see Marcus lying with the boy. They're both asleep, and I watch for a while as the blue light from between the slats creeps across the floor toward them, slowly moving from dark to light to white as it starts to touch his face. Ji Yoen trembles for a moment, his hand closing around my ribcage, then relaxes.

I swore to follow Marcus a long time ago. His was the first face I saw that wanted to pull me from the burned-out husk of the town. His hand came down through the pile of rubble that had once been my house and pulled me away. When the bomb that I'd been waiting for finally hit the house, I was happy, because it took the soldier who had been using me instead of his wife for what he would call "play time," too. I spent three days under that rubble lying on top of his dead body, afraid the entire time. Not of dying, but that he'd wake up. My greatest fear was that he would have survived and that the whole thing would start over again.

Now that he had been with the boy, the boy was one of us. Not that we all got along. Though I love Firuz, he and I have never really gotten along. With any group, there is always the chance of personality clash. Still, I would protect his life with mine. This Aaron Miller, though—he is too pure. Too young.

"Beloved," Abeo whispers.

"How long have you been watching me?" I whisper in return.

"Long enough," his beautiful eyes shift from mine to the couch and then back. "Why does he bother you so?"

"He doesn't bother me," I whisper.

Abeo laughs, closing his eyes. He pulls himself in closer, as if trying to burrow inside me. "Why does he bother you so?" he whispers again.

"It is possible that Marcus could fall for this one. Love this one."

Abeo does not look as he whispers, "Yes, but he has loved all of us in turn. Did it bother you so much when he loved me?"

"We all loved you."

"But you do not love this boy."

With his usual insight, Abeo had cut right to the heart. "No," I whispered, "I do not."

"What will you do?" Ji Yoen whispers.

"I am sorry to have woken you," I whisper in my poor Korean that he has labored hours to try to teach me.

"Answer," he whispers, using the command form of the verb. Abeo, who has already mastered it in the time I have taken to learn what a small child should know, grins. Like many of us, he can remember when Ji Yoen arrived, a frail, pitiful thing, afraid to even speak conditionally, let alone demand anything.

"I don't know," I whisper in English.

Little by little, they drift back to sleep. I am left alone, again, staring at the couch at the far end of the room and thinking that I am already seeing my doom.

MARCUS

File 2618-69370-B
Index: 9-06:41
Room 1159B
Transcript follows:

Harper: Good morning. We confirmed what you've told us. On behalf of the department, I want to thank you for your cooperation, and let you know that this has been noted in the file the judge will see.
(sounds of laughter)

Harper: What's funny?

Prisoner: Judge. As if this is a trial.

Harper: It is.

Prisoner: Please, Agent Harper. Let's not bullshit one another.
Harper: Look, the methods may not be the exact same as someone going through an investigation out there, but this is all still legal and done by the numbers, I can assure you.

Prisoner: As so many are fond of reminding the world on their social media, the Holocaust was perfectly legal, Agent Harper. You saying that what is happening here is legal is no comfort to me.

Harper: Well, that's your own business, then, I suppose. You know, it's funny in a way we've spent all this time talking and you've yet to tell me what this is all really about.

Prisoner: Untrue.

Harper: What, that this is really some crusade against straight people? Do you really believe that shit?

Prisoner: It seems like shit to you because of where you stand.

Harper: What does that mean?

Prisoner: If you don't understand, there's no way I can make you. It takes violence to get through to you people.

Harper: "You people." Do you hear yourself?

Prisoner: Do you hear what I'm saying?

Harper: Pretend for a second we're just two guys talking what's the point of this whole thing? (a long silence) Indulge me.

Prisoner: Leelah Alcorn, Jamey Rodemeyer, Carlos Vigil, Tyler Clementi, Taylor Alesana

Harper: I don't understand. Who are these people, these names?

Prisoner: The fact that you don't know who they are proves my point.

Harper: Were they associates of yours? Other people in your group?

Prisoner: They are the hallowed dead, the saints who show us the way. They, and the hundreds of thousands like them, and the hundreds of thousands who came before, are the reason we have to do what we do.

Harper: Who are they?
Prisoner: Each was a beautiful life, a person who was hounded simply because they weren't straight. Each eventually felt there was no other way out than suicide. Your people did that. Yours

Harper: Look, I don't see that

Prisoner: So when you come in here and throw twenty deaths at my feet and expect me to weep, I laugh. You have slaughtered (sound of pounding on metal) and

hounded (again, pounding on metal) my kind for millennia. All of those young people who had potential to be anything, to do anything, and because of their sexual orientation, they are now gone. You and your kind didn't give a shit about them. But these, these fucking people you do care about because they were sitting in a fucking church watching two straight people get married. You ask me about Aaron Miller? Aaron Miller died a fucking hero. Those people in at the wedding? They're the criminals.
(silence for a long time)

Harper: I can see that we're not going to get anywhere today. That'll be all.

AARON

7:54 pm

In_The_Shadows_42: I'm coming over tomorrow. There's something I want to ask you.
Idontknowwhattoputhere12: Okay, mystery man.
In_The_Shadows_42: ;)
Idontknowwhattoputhere12: What is it you want to ask?
In_The_Shadows_42: Too late now 5 minute warning.
Idontknowwhattoputhere12: Sometimes I really dislike your family
In_The_Shadows_42: Someday we'll have a house all our own, and we can talk as late as

late as we want

maybe even 8:15!
Idontknowwhattoputhere12: Do we dare dream of such a thing?
In_The_Shadows_42: Goodnight.
Idontknowwhattoputhere12: Goodnight

"So," I asked. "What is it you wanted to ask me?"

He's been here for almost ten minutes. We came upstairs and he sat down on my bed but didn't say anything.

His shorts are two sizes too big and slide far down on his hips. I can make out the top of his hip bone, and the smooth skin just above it. He's wearing a tank top that used to be dark gray but has faded almost brown. The picture on the front is of the band U2. It's way too big for him, and I can see all kinds of things that I think I shouldn't see, but I don't want to stop seeing. His arms are much thinner than I thought they were, but it makes me feel something in my chest—he's so little that I want to protect him. Like I want to slide my arms up under all those loose clothes and pull him to me. A few stray hairs from his armpit stick out, and some part of my brain says that I should think that's gross, but instead it makes my heart melt. It's not that I'm into doing weird things to armpits, or thinking about doing weird things with armpits...

It's—complicated.

It's like, being able to see parts of him that no one else really gets to see makes me feel special. That he's comfortable enough with me to let me see those things which would normally be carefully tucked away, it touches me. I reach out and I put my hand on the top of his arm. He turns his chair to face me.

Then he leans over, and as if he's known what I was thinking the whole time, kisses me.

Just like that. Like it's the easiest thing in the world.

My heart is pounding so hard against my chest that I'm sure he can feel it. The softness of his lips against mine, his hand on my thigh. We stayed like that, pressing against one another, for what felt like forever. He leaned back away from me a bit and stared directly into my eyes. Then he smiled and every bit of tension in my body just went away.

"So...have you, you know, *been* with anyone?" I ask.

"You mean like, what?" he replied.

I stare at him for a second, trying to think about how to phrase it better.

"Oh!" he said. "Oh." He plays with his shoelace for a second. "I guess. I mean, I dunno. There's this whole big conversation about what counts and what doesn't, you know?"

"Oh, yeah," I said, playing it off.

"Do you mean, like, sucking a guy off? Or do you mean more?"

"Either," I said, trying desperately to not seem shocked.

"I guess...there was this guy back in my old neighborhood. I liked him. We would hang out when he wasn't out with his friends or with his girlfriend or whatever. I blew him a few times," he said.

"Did you like him?" I asked.

"I dunno. I mean, I wanted to be with him and whatever, but as soon as we were done, I just kind of wanted him to leave. We didn't cuddle or anything."

A moment stretched out between us. "So," he said, "yeah. But I haven't really done anything...you know, not anything else." He looks over at me, "What about you?"

I had a decision to make at that point. I hadn't ever done anything but jerk off ever. I mean, I'd imagined some pretty crazy stuff, to be honest, but at that point, my entire sexual history could be summed up as "flying solo." I mean, I knew enough to know that I didn't have to be ashamed about the actual wank, but I knew that at my age, I should have maybe at least tried to have someone else involved. At least, that's what everyone else seemed to be saying to me all the time. But should I lie about it? I mean, I'd seen lots of movies where the high school guy lies about his ability and then gets in the moment and has no idea what to do. I wasn't sure that we were headed that way, but I knew that if we did, I'd be lost. It's one thing to imagine how tab A fits into slot B, but quite another to assemble a dining room table.

I made a decision, "No. I mean, I want to, but I just...you know... haven't."

"Oh," he said, smiling. "That's cool," he says, and puts his hand on my knee. Then he leans in and kisses me. I kept thinking to myself,

"Remember this, remember this, remember this, remember this" but it happened so fast that I couldn't tell you what his leaning in was like, or how he smelled, or the first touch of his lips on mine. All I knew was that one minute we were talking, and the next minute my shirt was off, he was lying against me, his hands were all over my body, and that his butt fit perfectly in my hands. I was sure that any second, I was going to split open my pants, but somehow never did.

He pulled back. Our eyes locked, and he smiled. "Okay?" he whispered. I nodded, and he pushes me a bit to lie on my back while he moves between my legs. I'd heard the phrase "dry humping" and I had a mental idea of what it was, but I wasn't ready for what it felt like. I used to think, "How could anyone get any pleasure out of that?" but it was like being hit with fireworks, each made out of pressure and moaning. My legs wrapped around his waist and my ankles locked behind him without me telling them to. It was like everything went on autopilot.

His lips tugged gently at my earlobe. "Wait," I whispered, "hang on...I'm about..." was all the warning I could give him before everything inside me exploded.

I had some pretty intense finishes to my sessions with myself. Once I even managed to shoot over my own head and hit the headboard of my bed. I thought I knew how intense the very most intense version of that feeling could be. I had, though, experienced absolutely nothing before that moment. My feet tensed so hard that they started to cramp. I'm sure I would have actually cried out if there had been any breath in my lungs at all.

I don't know how much time passed with me just lying there, spasming again and again into my underwear, while he slowly pushed against me and I felt his breathing in my ear, but it felt like days. He leaned back on his knees and my legs dropped to the bed, though, finally, and even though my closed eyes, I knew he was smiling. I opened them to look at him, and that's when I saw the clock.

Start to finish, the whole thing had taken 4 minutes. I looked back at him, "I'm sorry," I said, just knowing that he was disappointed by how quickly things had ended. I'd waited my whole life to have sex, to see another person naked on purpose, to feel all the things that books and movies had promised me about having someone inside me, and it was all over before either of us even had our pants off.

"For what?" he said, smiling.

"That it was so...you know..."

"Quick?" he said, but something in his tone told me he was teasing. "I think of it as a compliment." And just like that, I completely relaxed. He put his hand on my hip, and his thumb moved just a bit.

Which is when I had time to look down at notice that his shorts were hardly containing him. I reached out and touched, and his eyes closed. I let my fingers move along the whole length, and some part of me realized he and I were about the same size, and relaxed. I hadn't even thought about it, but some part of me had been worried that I'd be with someone who was bigger, and that they'd laugh at the size of mine.

"Can..." I started to say, "Can I...?"

He nodded, and I unbuttoned his shorts. I pulled his zipper down, then slid the front of his boxer briefs down. It was pointing straight up, and for a second it moved. I realized it was throbbing with his pulse. I hadn't ever seen mine do that. It was smoother than mine, and the head was bigger around, but flatter, somehow. His hair was curlier.

"Do you want to...?" he asked, looking down at me.

And I did. I did want to. I was just about to put it in my mouth when we both heard the front door open, though, and close.

"Aaron?" came my mom's voice from downstairs.

He rolled immediately onto his side and had his zipper up and button buttoned almost instantly. As I slid my shirt on and brushed at my hair with my fingers, I wondered how he'd gotten so expert at that move. We both moved to where we'd been sitting before just as my bedroom door opened.

"Oh, there you are," my mom said, "Hello, Daniel. Aaron, come help me get the groceries out of the car." As I stood up, I hoped there'd been enough time for my second erection, which had come as quite a surprise to me, to go down. I turned sideways to her. "Is Daniel staying for dinner?" she asked.

"I gotta' go," he said. I didn't want him to, but I knew if he didn't in that very second we might somehow give the whole thing away to her.

It took everything I had in me to let go of his hand as he walked out the bedroom door and downstairs.

7:51 pm

Idontknowwhattoputhere12: Do you guys ever finish dinner before it's too late to talk?
In_The_Shadows_42: Sorry
Idontknowwhattoputhere12: So, are we
Idontknowwhattoputhere12: together?
In_The_Shadows_42: Yes.
Idontknowwhattoputhere12: Wow.
In_The_Shadows_42: What?
Idontknowwhattoputhere12: That was just really fast. You didn't hesitate at all.
In_The_Shadows_42: Should I have?
Idontknowwhattoputhere12: No. I didn't want you to. This is all just as;lkdjfjls
In_The_Shadows_42: For me, too.
Idontknowwhattoputhere12: I want you to stay

In_The_Shadows_42: I'm not going anywhere.

Idontknowwhattoputhere12: No, I mean I want you to stay over. With me.

In_The_Shadows_42: Oh.

Idontknowwhattoputhere12: If you don't want to, I guess that's

In_The_Shadows_42: No, I do. It's just going to take some doing.

Idontknowwhattoputhere12: With the parents?

In_The_Shadows_42: Yeah. I've never really asked to. Or at least not in a while.

Idontknowwhattoputhere12: But you do want to?

In_The_Shadows_42: Yes (5 minute warning). I'll start working on it on this side.

Idontknowwhattoputhere12: I will, too. On this side, I mean. Work on it.

In_The_Shadows_42: I have to go. Goodnight.

Idontknowwhattoputhere12: Goodnight.

It took some wrangling (with my mom), some lying (to his parents), and more than a bit of wheedling on both our parts, but a few nights later, Daniel was sleeping over. What is funny to me now, looking back, is that I don't even really remember the sex as much as I remember the time after. We were both completely naked and lying on top of the sheets. Decadent wasn't a word I used ever, really, but that was the feeling—as if we had time, as if we would never be interrupted by something as stupid as life ever again. We'd separated for just a bit and were holding hands because we were both overheated, but after a few moments of panting, he laid his head on my chest and wrapped his left leg over the top of my legs. His forehead rested just against my lips.

At that moment, I thought to myself that I had a concept of what relaxed meant before that very moment, and that concept had just expanded until I realized I'd never relaxed before in my life until then.

He laughed.

"What?" I asked.

"Nothing," he said, and his left hand wrapped around my right arm.

"No, what?" I asked.

"Nothing, It's stupid."

"Tell me."

"I just figured out why they call them body pillows, is all."

We both laughed.

"I'm thirsty, but I can't move," I said.

"Same," he whispered.

"So this was your first?" I asked, though looking back, I don't know what made me ask.

He nodded his head against me, "Yours, too, right?" he asked.

"Yeah," I said.

For so many people in the world that kind of special never happens, or when it does it passes without much thought. I know that now. Then, though, we both just lay there letting that moment stretch out between us.

"Sometimes," he said looking upward at the ceiling as light from a car pulling into the parking lot swept across the window, "I think that things are so bad, so terrible with the hate on the TV and the radio, the wars that won't ever end, and it gets easy to think that it's all too terrible to deal with. But then something happens and the whole thing seems almost beautiful."

"Even the hate?"

"Well, I mean, I don't like that people openly hate us on TV or that kids get taken to camps and beaten until they say they want to marry a woman or whatever. I didn't mean that. I just meant that, here, with you like this, there's good, too," he said. "Like, if we could hover over the planet up in orbit for a second, just for a second, the whole thing would make sense. There's hate and war and death, but there's also love and sex and kittens."

"Kittens?" I asked, hoping he could hear the smile in my voice.

"Mmmhm," he said, nuzzling into me once more.

A few weeks went by and we were together more and no matter how horrible things might get, we could always find that space in my room, tangled together, where there was peace. I was naïve enough to think it might go on forever like that.

Wouldn't that be something.

VIKTOR

Marcus talks about the new day that is coming. The dawning of something. The others listen to him, and you can see the worship in their eyes. And I want to feel that way, too.

I just don't.

To me, this all feels like the end of something. Like we're at the tail end of a chance, and it's slipping through our fingers. Every day, images of white, middle-class families with five kids, happy. They like the world that they see. And why shouldn't they? It gives them everything they want. It congratulates them for who they are and how they think, feel, act.

It's their world.

All they want is for us to go away. To their minds, that's not such a big request. Just stop talking about inequality and yelling about our rights and stop coming out of the closet and throwing our existence in their faces. They don't want to have to have complicated conversations with their kids. They don't want their kids to think that what we do is okay.

Give us this day our daily opportunity to pretend the whole world is like us so that we can concentrate on what matters, like which major Hollywood starlet is fucking what producer, and how to spend less on shoes.

I think about the plan while Marcus talks, the others listening to him, spellbound, and I wonder if it will make a difference. The world will pause for maybe 12 hours, then we will be nothing more than a curiosity for the next few days. Eventually we'll fade from the news cycle entirely. There'll be one more story a year from now, a memorial. One of those idiots will probably turn it into a fundraiser for some conservative cause, giving the money raised to some thinly veiled campaign to put another conservative in the White House.

For it to make any difference it will have to escalate.

"Hello," Marcus says to me. I had been so lost in my own thought I hadn't heard him stop talking, dismiss everyone, and walk over to me.

"Hello," I say, looking away from him. He puts his hands just above my elbows and pulls me close.

"It's you," he says. I look into his eyes. Sensing my confusion, he says, "they've picked you to start the next step."

"Okay," I nod. But it isn't. We both know what this means.

"Okay," he says, his thumb caressing my arm. When he lets go and walks away, it's hard for me to stay standing.

"What was that?" Ji Yoen asks after a moment.

"When there is any major action, someone has to stay behind just in case the action fails. If it looks like everyone is going to be captured, that person has to be responsible for contacting the next group, for activating them."

"Okay," Ji Yoen says.

I'm still watching down the hall as Marcus stops at his bedroom door, looks up at me, then goes in and shuts the door behind him.

"That person is always picked by someone higher up so that it's never about relationships or anything personal. Always just random," I said. "This time, it's me."

"Isn't that a good thing?" Ji Yoen asks.

"It means I won't be there with you if something goes wrong. Marcus will, but I won't."

"Oh," Ji Yoen says, and by his tone of voice, I can tell he understands, now.

AARON

It sounds dirty and cheap to say it like this, but Daniel and I had sex many more times. I want to say something like "made love," but to me that sounds worse. I don't know that there's a word for what we were, how it was dirty and lustful and clean and beautiful all at the same time. I'm sure everyone feels that way, that what they do is somehow special, but that's how it felt. I knew it was related to the porn I'd seen, but that it felt infinitely different.

I'll be honest, while all of that was amazing, and having someone touch parts of me that I never thought any one else would ever touch was incredible, even more incredible because it was Daniel doing that touching, what I really liked was the after. The time after that seemed to slip between the seconds of the clock, almost like a bubble. The time when we were both still naked, but holding one another, and talking in a way I'd never talked before, where sound and touch and breathing were just as important as words. I hated when we had to get up and sneak to the bathroom separately to get cleaned off and then get dressed. We'd always go right back to our cuddle, but it was different, somehow. It was a part of the regular world where minutes passed.

In those weeks, we also ran into Marcus a few times, always being invited back to his house for dinner or tea. He would always serve us teas with exotic and impressive names that, no matter how hard I looked, I could never find in the grocery store. The talk was on the same topics, always; did we know about the ways authors of classic pieces of literature used code words or phrases to show the audience that two characters were in a relationship together? When we said no, he would go on a tear about something called compulsory heterosexuality and how it impacted education. Did we know that as many as 40% of entertainers in the music industry were gay but had the demand that they could not come out of the closet put into their contracts by major record labels? Did we know that most hip-hop artists who were gay and even hinted at trying to come out wound up shot? And of course, the answer was always no. We didn't know these things. Did we know about how many world leaders were gay but had to keep a wife or a husband as a beard in order to throw off the straight-controlled political parties?

To be honest, during that time, I not only didn't know most of what Marcus told us, I found myself not caring much. My only thoughts were about Daniel. Marcus didn't care how much touching and hand holding and sitting in each others' laps we did while in his place as long as we were listening. I think much of the reason we wound up accepting his invitations when they came was so that we could have that time to be physically intimate with one another.

Marcus would always end one of our visits by saying Daniel should do a video about these things. And I honestly think Daniel meant to, it's just that we were in the early stages of a relationship, and we weren't thinking about much other than each other.

Did I wonder, sometimes, why we could never go to Daniel's house to hang out? Why he never invited me over? I think maybe I did, but again—what was there other than the necessity of finding places to be alone together? What else but his lips and hands could possibly be important?

Another night in that sweet later that new relationships exist within, timeless and eternal. Him lying against me, arm around my chest, the smell of us in the air. Our hearts beating next to one another.

"So, I think I want to do the boyfriend tag," Daniel said.

"I've seen some of those. Isn't it a bit..."

"A bit what?" Daniel asked.

"I dunno. Isn't it a bit old? Like, done to death?"

"Hmmm," was all he said but snuggled in closer.

"So, what do you think of him?" Daniel asked.

"Think of who?" I asked in return.

"Marcus."

"I don't know, really. I hadn't thought much about him."

"Hmm," Daniel said, his arm moving down to my ribcage and pull me closer to him.

"Why? What do you think about him?"

"I think he's a bit...extreme," Daniel whispered.

"Hmm," I mumbled.

"I worry," Daniel said.

"About?"

"I don't know. I guess, People like that. In the world. What they can wind up doing."

"Do you want to stop hanging out with him?" I asked.

"Maybe," Daniel said.

After that we drifted off together.

My Mom agreed to let me go to see Winston Mendez, the guy that Daniel told me about. I hated lying to her about it, but I just wasn't ready to tell her what was going on. She thought the guy was some kind of motivational speaker. Even that took some convincing, though. I told her that my new friend, Daniel, was way into this whole motivational speaking thing. If she had looked him up at all she would have seen right through my lie, but she was busy, too. I also may have implied that at least one of Daniel's parents was going to be going. In my defense, I never directly said they were, just that, "we're going in Daniel's dad's car." That part was technically not a lie—

Daniel put on a corduroy sport that he'd gotten from Goodwill and borrowed his dad's little hatchback.

I just thought that there would be time to clear all this up, later. To finally tell her and admit to all of this and let her yell a little and come to some kind of new balance.

I'd never been downtown, really. I mean, Mom and I had passed through on our way to other places, so I knew what it looked like, but this was my first time being there. It seemed so huge, empty, and a little frightening. We walked through the enormous parking lot toward the huge events center. Luckily, the place was lit well and the staff were on the lookout for people just like us, young folks looking lost. Everyone smiled and helped us find our seats.

"People seem so friendly," Daniel said. I nodded to show that I was surprised by it, too. I had lived the past few days with a vague dread of people, including the staff at the events center, being rude. When they weren't, I was not only happy, I felt somehow lighter. We saw gay couples our own age and one or two even younger. T-shirts that said, "Some men have vaginas—deal with it," or "Here. Queer. Deal." Everywhere rainbow flags. It was like a black and white film suddenly having color.

The crowd was enormous. I'd never seen this many people all gathered together in one spot before. The crowd started cheering when a woman in a black suit and tie stepped out onto the stage but settled quickly. Daniel held my hand on his lap.

"Good evening," she said. "I'm Doctor Martha Lone Hill from the university, and I want to start by thanking you all for coming out tonight." The crowd got loud again, and I got goosebumps. I felt a part of something. "Given everything that has happened over the last decade, it is important for us to support speakers like our guest tonight, and to make sure that now, more than ever, we are all speaking up for our rights as lesbian, gay, bisexual, and transgender people." A cheer, bigger than the first two, erupted from the crowd. Doctor Lone Hill stepped back from the microphone and nodded, waiting. "We must make sure that the ultraconservatives that came in on the Thompson ticket are not the only voices that mainstream America is hearing. And so it is with great pleasure that I bring to you tonight one of the biggest voices we have right now, one of our most outspoken allies, Winston Mendez," she said and gestured offstage.

The man who came out looked younger than my mom. He was also in a black suit and tie, but his hair was spiky and cool. I actually had to put my hands over my ears to drown out the cheer that came as he stepped up to the microphone and waited, smiling. At one point, his eyes swept over us in the upper deck, and for just a second, I could have sworn he was looking right at me. It felt like forever before the cheer died down but my watch said it had only been four minutes.

"Thank you," he said, gesturing palms-down for us to settle. "Thank you so much. Thank you. Oh, you're too kind. Thank you. Thank you."

Once we'd all settled, he started:

"As many of you know, I'm very fond of Wonder Woman. What an amazing icon. What a powerful character," he said, and paused while we all applauded and whistled. "Most people, when they think about her, think about a statuesque ass kicker in those patriotic hot pants. That's what they remember. And if that's what they remember, that's not bad. We could do worse than to have a powerful female role model in that masculine sense of power through violence.

"But what many don't think about is that she was an emissary for her people. The representative of an ancient group of female warriors to the world that is run by men. She comes from outside with a message of peace through harmony of the sexes. And all this was invented in the character before the famous Women's Lib movement, just to give credit where credit's due.

"I like that idea. I like the idea of someone from the outside bringing a message to the mainstream. So, I hope you don't mind that I'm bringing a bit of her up here with me," he said, and stepped aside the podium. He hiked up his suit pants just a bit to show that he had on blue high-top Chuck Taylors. The camera zooms in and, on the huge television screen above, we can all see that his shoes have Wonder Woman on them. He came wearing his Wonder Woman high-tops.

We all laugh, and there is applause and whistling. Someone yells, "We love you!" I look over at Daniel and take his hand. He squeezes mine softly.

Winston steps back behind the podium. "So, she's here with us this evening. A bit of strength to help me, like her, bring my message to the outside world.

"See, I, too, come from this amazing line of women warriors. If there's one thing all my critics can agree on, it's that I was privileged to have grown up in such a safe space. They often say that like my luck in that regard negates whatever I can say. They're right in that one regard—I was very lucky. And I know that. And part of the reason I do these tours, and put out the books, is to deliver the messages that I was given back to all of you. ALL of us. Gay, Bi, Trans, Queer, Questioning, Asexual, and all the million other colors of the rainbow that I didn't just mention. ALL of us." Again, the auditorium erupted in applause, whistling, more people yelling their love.

"My mom, a righteous warrior woman from the heart of the 60s, which she always called 'The Front Line' of the struggle for all of us—white, black, LGBT, straight, women, men—she said to me when I was just a little sprout, 'Son,' she said, 'at some point, you're going to have the choice I wasn't given: to speak up, to stand up and by standing and speaking, to raise the consciousness of the entire world, or' she said, 'to go about your daily life quietly, trying to get your needs and only your needs met. When you are given that choice, I know what I'd want you to do, but you have to make that choice yourself.' You see, she gave me the choice.

"What I didn't understand at the time, and am only just now coming to see, is that we make that choice every day. It wasn't just a one-time choice. We make that choice every day. All of us. And in raising me the way she did, she was giving me all the tools to do either thing. Many of you have read my mother's books, seen her in news footage, you know that she was a powerful speaker in public. But what most don't know is how gentle and quiet she was at home. You see, she was showing me both things. That a warrior should not always be at war and that a civilian can take up arms for a cause they believe in when they choose to.

"That's what I'm here today to talk about. A kind of direct answer to my critics who keep saying that I'm somehow not a good model for how someone who claims to speak for us all should be, because I was lucky enough to have two moms, one of which was a second wave feminist icon, and the other, a successful business owner. To be honest, sometimes I do think that they have a point. But then sometimes I think they're mad because they weren't the ones being interviewed by *Rolling Stone*. But much like Wonder Woman, I say that my training outside what most people experienced leads me to have unique insights. And that I can share those insights with all of you to go and use in your daily lives, that you can use to make your choices every day.

"So, before we move forward, can we agree that I'm not here to tell you how much better I am than you? Can we agree that my upbringing was very lucky, and that my coming out process was very smooth compared to most of yours, but that I'm not here to brag about those things? That just because I choose not to spend my time in bars doesn't mean I look down on any of you who have found family and comfort in those bars? That because I don't do drugs doesn't mean that I look down on those of you who feel you have to in order to make it through the terrible hand you may have been dealt? Before we move forward, can we agree that I'm not here to tell you how much better I am than you, but instead to show you how we're all the same, and that, together, we can all come together and make all of our lives better? Can we agree on that?" By that point, the swell in applause and cheers and whistles and noise had grown so much that the people in charge of sound had to raise the volume of the microphone. On the last question his voice was rattling my ribcage. I looked at Daniel, and he was smiling and crying.

"Cisgenderist," Winston says after the noise dies down. "That's what they call me, too. They say it with the same tone as they would 'traitor.' They say that I don't do enough to combat transphobia. That somehow or another, simply because I'm not transgender, I must have bought into the homophobic web of institutions that surrounds us, traps us all to the wheel," Here, he paused and shook his head. Again, cries of love, a few shouts of disbelief.

"The other day, I was volunteering, and I was sitting close enough to two young men to hear their conversation. Now, eavesdropping is not a nice thing to do, but there were so many of us trying to help that day that there was no way not to overhear what people were saying. The coffee wasn't that great, either," he says and flashes a grin that makes all of us smile, too. He looks offstage, and we can all tell that whoever he aimed that ribbing at probably grinned, too. We all laugh.

"But we were all there, volunteering, instead of dying behind the giant wall of apathy that they use to keep us all docile. These two young men were helping fold information letters and put them in envelopes. We've all been there, right? It's shitty work," he says, and pauses, and looks back offstage quickly, "Uh oh. Jim? Jim? Am I allowed to say 'shit?'" There's a pause while, presumably someone named Jim answers him. He flashes that huge smile, again, and shrugs. "He says, 'well, you already did it, and no one has stormed into the control room to shut us down. so I guess we're good.'" The whole crowd laughs. Again, cheers, whistling.

"So these two young guys were talking about their boyfriends. And one of them says to the other, 'I think things would be different, though, if only he wasn't so…I dunno…faggy.'" He pauses. "'Faggy,' this young man said." Here, he steps out from behind the podium and walks a few steps, shaking his head. "Instead of stopping his friend, and having a conversation about what he meant, the second young man said that his boyfriend was, and I'm quoting again, 'pretty queeny, too.' They both laughed and began having a conversation about their respective boyfriend's most 'faggy' and 'queeny' habits. Through that conversation I came to understand that they were bewildered and often ashamed by their boyfriends' stereotypically feminine behaviors. Stereotypically Western feminine behaviors, I should also point out, as there are plenty of tribes, nations, and so forth, in which what is expected behavior from the female, however that is defined in that particular culture, is what people in Branson, Missouri, would call downright manly," he says, grinning again.

Somehow, though, I felt that his grin was less powerful, here. That, somehow, the force of these two young men's misstep had wilted him a bit.

"I get why some in the heteronormative world might be uninformed enough to make that assumption, that the stereotypically feminine is the thing to be rooted out and destroyed on sight. But these were two young gay men. I know because during the course of the conversation, both of them self-identified to one another as that very thing. Not only young gay men, but young gay men awake enough, compassionate enough, to be volunteering their time at a local nonprofit. Perhaps it was stereotyping of a different kind, but I think perhaps we can expect a bit more aware behavior from people in that position. Yet, here these two young men were, talking about their boyfriends—not even idly gossiping about some random strangers, but instead insulting their closest mate, their best friend of best friends, their boyfriends." The way he says it makes me turn to Daniel. Daniel is already staring at me, and there are tears in his eyes, again. He squeezes my hand.

"For how long now?" he asks, and pauses, again.

"For how long now have we endured this fear? This need to find and root out all that is stereotypically feminine in ourselves as a way of appeasing the straight, sexist, heteronormative, cisgenderist world? We who know better, mind you, still gathering around, using sexism and the rest of that cocktail of hatred as a yardstick. We who know better, still giving power to a system that tells us that Arnold Schwarzenegger's impregnable body and Bruce Willis' emotionless banter is the goal, and anything less than that means we might as well have a vagina. Because that system tells us that having a vagina is a bad thing. That anything that system defines as feminine is a poison, and that our goal must be to dig it out of ourselves and burn it on a pyre for all to see. This they call strength. It's bad enough that straight men march around, constantly performing their little dance of conformity to that system for each other. But aren't we?...my friends, aren't we who have been nothing but victimized by that silly dance...don't we already know better?

"For how long now have we endured this fear of theirs, whether we were born with a body that felt comfortable or confining, whether we were born finding it easy to hide within their system or not, whether we fit neatly into their column A or column B or felt nothing but the imprisonment that system represents, how long have we endured the torture and the beatings and the wagging tongues because we, who know better, are still using their yardstick for our own lives?" The energy in the room swells like there's going to be another round of "I love yous," but none come.

"My friends, the goal is not to have us all become every letter in our rainbow alphabet. Some are comfortable as beings who blur any category line that they come within ten feet of and bless them. They're amazing. Truly, they are. But the goal is not for all of us to politicize our sex, nor for us to sexualize our politics. Unless that's your thing, then by all means, become moral pornographers, as Angela Davis suggests.

"However, can we at least all agree that we need to stop attacking one another based on a yardstick that is not only rooted in childish misunderstanding, but also isn't meant for us? Can we at least agree on that? As I've said in other places, and received no end of grief for, as I'm sure you know, coming out in high school wasn't an experience I had. For me, the dice that were rolled at my birth turned out favorably, according to that old yardstick. Without having to try too hard, I was fairly comfortable in my skin as a boy. I had fairly stereotypically masculine behaviors without having to try to hard to put them in place. While many would have you believe that because of this, something essential to the cause was missing, and I shouldn't be listened to," he says, and the chorus of boos, and shouts starts to swell, but he brings up his hand, and it dies slowly back down, "They may be right. Maybe. But let me tell you about Donald.

"I've talked about Donald in other interviews, but I want to talk about it, here, too. Donald was another boy in the same year in my school. I didn't know him very well because we just didn't run in the same circles. As I have said many times, I hope that Donald is out there, and that he's doing well. After high school ended, and we all went off to discover what utter bullshit high school was, I lost track of him. For Donald at that age, though, nothing about gender or sexuality seemed to come easy. He was one of millions of LGBTQQIA kids who cannot pass. The demands of that stupid yardstick are simply too much.

"Every day, from the vantage point of safety, I watched Donald's struggle. And I wanted to help him, but even then I knew, or at least intuited, that high school was a crisis situation. Like a plane crash. If you've paid attention during the safety speech at the beginning of every flight...I know, I know, who has time? You have to remember, I was born during an era when you still had to turn your electronics off before the plane could even taxi, let alone take off. Back when we had to dodge dinosaurs to take a shuttle to Des Moines," he says, and grins again. We all relax a bit. "In that little speech, they say that, in the event of an emergency, the oxygen mask will drop from the ceiling. When it does, they say, you have to put your own mask on first, then help anyone else around you with theirs if they are having trouble.

"Back then, I couldn't have articulated this very well, but I knew that, if I was going to survive the worst mistake the education of human beings has ever produced, i.e. the high school system in America, I had to try to get my own mask on first. And, you see, that's the horrible beauty of the system they've devised. Reaching out to help someone else? That's coded as feminine behavior. No matter how big Captain America's muscles are, sticking up for the little guy? That's how you ring the dinner bell for the sharks in the water.

"So, even as I had the fantastic sex life of a closeted football player, and let me tell you, it was something else. Teenage sexuality is volatile to say the least, and when you combine the right symbols, like a uniform, with the right behaviors, such as a seeming ease of masculinity, people do things that they never would at any other time in their lives. But even as that was going on, young men who had just finished having sex with me would make fun of Donald. As if, somehow, they could define themselves as 'not-that' by rejecting Donald. His stereotypically feminine behaviors, combined with his seeming lack of desire to even try to hide himself, his lack of acknowledgement that the yardstick ruled his life, formed, for them, an important barrier.

"What am I getting at, here?" he says, pausing, pacing back toward the podium. "Why bring all this up? What I'm getting at is so simple that we reject it because it seems too simple. We reject it because we feel that the answer must be more complicated. But it isn't. You," he says, and points to all of us. On the giant television, his finger seems to be pointing directly at me. For a second, I panic, as if he wants me to stand up and explain myself. "You, sitting right here, and me, all of us—we have to stop attacking each other based on the yardstick. We have to let go of that system if we're going to get anywhere. Not only not hold on to it, but to reject that it ever meant anything at all. That is not to say that we must all become pansexual, fluidly-gendered beings—though perhaps we already are—but instead, that we have to stop equating whether or not we fit with an arbitrary system of gender with our value. You, sitting right there, and me, and all of us, it doesn't matter if we like to crochet, it doesn't matter if we like beer or not, it doesn't matter if we feel more comfortable at the bridal shower than what some Brits call the 'Stag Do.' It doesn't matter, and we have to stop beating ourselves, and each other, up for it.

"So, to the people who attack me based on the fact that I happen to have masculine behaviors, and that I had the choice about whether or not to come out in high school, and that I chose not to, what I will say is, let go of their system of oppression. Let us not oppress each other using their tools. Our behavior must be different." He looks down at the podium for a second, long enough that we can all tell he's reading something.

"Our behavior towards ourselves, toward each other, it must be different. Can we at least agree on that? I hear young people every day tell me that they don't want to be put in a box, that they don't want to be labeled. At the same time, others have looked long and hard to find their people, and once they find them, they become fiercely proud of that label, like a battleflag. How do we bridge this gap?

"Those young gay men I talked about earlier, they also spent some time speculating about another friend of theirs who told them he was bisexual. They seemed quite in doubt, and insisted to one another that bisexuality was a myth. People in one of the categories oppressing someone else in another category, as if somehow LGBTQQAI is not all written on the same line, but instead as a hierarchy. Please tell me you can see the problem there. How do we bridge this gap? How do we ask the out to have more compassion for the closeted without asking them to devalue the struggle they've lived through in coming out? How do we bridge this gap?

"I must admit, my friends," he says, his shoulders sagging, "I don't know. I don't know. But I do know how we start, at least. And that might be all we need for now. How do we start?

"We listen to each other. Instead of finding reasons to reject one another, be it that old yardstick, or some other even more arbitrary system, we listen to one another. And if someone's idea about themselves, or the world, doesn't mesh with yours, instead of responding as if they've threatened you, how about nodding, and saying 'I may not agree, but I respect what you're saying.' Maybe that's the key; instead of doing what the oligarchs and the hegemons, the politicians and the priests, those who wish us nothing but harm want, which is to fight each other, maybe we stop fighting long enough to listen. To respect each other's differences without thinking that those differences destroy any chances of similarity.

"We all know that the family you are born into is not the one almost any of us would choose. I have a friend who actually breaks out in hives every time the holidays roll around. But we've all had the experience of choosing a family for ourselves. Of populating our inner circle with people we trust.

"What if the way we start to bridge the gaps is to decide, not by accident, not from lack of choice, but actively decide that we are each other's family? What if," he says, and stepped from behind the podium again, looking at the stage, his hand in mid-gesture. "What if," he said, again, turning to the audience. I watched the giant television screen above the stage as it zoomed in on his smile. It was dazzling, and when his eyes happened to sweep in the direction of the camera, it looked like he was smiling directly at me. Like a great god of mercy was looking at me with all of his attention and loving me. My eyes grew blurry.

It was because they were so blurry that I didn't see exactly how he reacted when the first bullet hit him. To be honest, I'm not even sure I knew that a shot had rung out. That part may be me inserting something into my memory after the fact that wasn't there to begin with.

When the second shot happened, though, my eyes were clear. I saw him jerk, and stumble back further on the stage. His chest was bloody, and he was clutching at his left arm. He fell backwards, and I found myself looking at the television screen rather than at the real thing happening on the stage. Because of that, I saw his head bounce when it hit the stage.

It was only at that moment that my brain caught up to what was happening, and I realized someone was shooting at Winston Mendez. That he'd been shot.

VIKTOR

I'm not going to tell you that I feel justified in every single action I've ever taken. There's this idea in some of us that, if there is a God, when we stand before him, we'll be able to hold our heads up high and answer for everything we've ever done. If God does exist, I know for a fact I won't be. This is why I hope that there truly isn't a God.

I do have limits. They are far outside what you would think of as the actions of a rational person, but they are limits just the same.

Daniel Young is about the same age I was when the soldiers first... noticed...me. That only makes all of this harder. I've watched more of his videos than I've told any of the others. In a different time, a different universe, he would be on talk shows as a young leader. Someone who stopped suicides and helped teachers understand what things were like for their gay students. He would be winning awards for being so young and yet so focused. Instead, he's trapped here, in this world, like the rest of us. The one where overfed old men try to recreate an earlier decade which they think was so much simpler but in reality wasn't. A world where straight people make all their decisions by thinking they are normal and we are somehow failed experiments who would have better lives if we could just accept Jesus into our hearts.

"We could just recruit him," I had said to Marcus early on. He had thought it was a good enough idea that we were already moved in and just about to start talking to the boy when the other orders came through.

X Winston Mendez X was all the text message had said. It would mean nothing to anyone, including us, but it came through on *that* phone. The one that only ever received messages, never sent them. And so, in an instant, we went from attempting to recruit to setting up for war.

What I didn't know at that time was that another message had come through: X St. Augustine Church X.

All I knew was that, for some reason, Marcus began talking to another boy living in the complex we'd moved into. Marcus, I know now, had already started to keep secrets from the rest of us. He'd already decided a course of action without consulting anyone, even me.

The night after Marcus pulled the trigger and killed Mendez we had angry, mean sex. This alarmed me, because he and I had never been anything but gentle and caring before. I had always thought that he couldn't have ever been anything like those soldiers, but that night he was. I went back into being a mouse, just like back then, and waited for it to be over. After he finished, we were lying side by side panting when he whispered, "Daniel."

"What?" I asked.

"Very soon, a day, a week maybe, I'm going to say that name again, and when I do, you will go and kill Daniel Young. You will make it look like a suicide."

"But I thought we were here to recruit him. His videos could become an asset to us."

"This comes from higher up. Now that Mendez is dead, we're going to kill Daniel, and then recruit Aaron."

I spent the next two days trying to make sense of an order like that, but it made no sense at all. We were supposed to be trying to liberate boys exactly like these two—why should I be trying to kill one of them?

Aaron was over quite a bit during that next week but without Daniel. It was hard to get a moment alone with Marcus. When I finally did, I pressed him further. "I am still unclear—why do you want to kill the boy? Why not just recruit him, and if you want the Miller boy, we can recruit him, too?"

"I don't ask the higher ups why they want a thing done. They say do and we do," Marcus said.

"Aren't we supposed to be helping boys just like this?"

He gave me a look that said he was finished talking about the subject and walked away.

As it turns out, the world was moving one step ahead of us.

MARCUS

File 2618-69370-B

Index: 10-08:41

Room 1159B

Transcript follows:

Harper: How many others?

Prisoner: Good morning to you, too.

Harper: I mean it if you want any more information about your little friend, you better start giving me information. I mean quick.

Prisoner: How many other what?

Harper: I've got potentials here that match St. Augustine in one way or another going back over two decades. How many?

Prisoner: I don't know how many.
(the sound of something hitting metal)

Harper: How many of these operations have you been a part of?

Prisoner: How is Viktor?

Harper: Uh uh, you don't get to know anything until you talk.

(quiet for almost three minutes)

Prisoner: Give me a list

(sounds of paper shuffling)

Harper: Any of these? If so, which?

Prisoner: This one. This. This one, too. And this. This one as well. And this. And this.

Harper: Jesus fucking Christ.

Prisoner: Turn the page for me please? (sound of paper) This. And this one. This one I was there for, but I wasn't part of the mission.

Harper: They killed the fucking

Prisoner: And this one. This one, too, but again, not as part of the crew. I was learning back then.

Harper: Unfuckingbelievable

Prisoner: Turn the page please? (sound of paper) No, these are too old. They were not me. Some of them I don't think are us, as well.

Harper: Which ones aren't your people?

Prisoner: First, how is Viktor?

Harper: (exhale) Still stable. Still critical. They think he'll be that way for a while. For a moment, they were considering medically-induced coma, but that's not an option anymore.

Prisoner: He is strong. He will live.

Harper: Now, which ones are you fairly sure weren't done by your people?

AARON

The word "assassin" feels too over the top to use in everyday conversation. Most people wouldn't say "assassinated" in a normal sentence. Somehow it feels like something that can only occur in the past. Lincoln was assassinated, Kennedy was assassinated, Martin Luther King, Jr, was assassinated. Most people don't think it's something that can happen right in front of their eyes.

But even as Daniel stood, his hand now clutching mine tightly, I knew that we'd just watched someone be assassinated.

There is a moment, small, fleeting, when nothing happens. Everyone freezes in place, like your grade school PE teacher used to get everyone to do by blowing a whistle. No one moved. No one spoke.

Then—chaos.

Screaming and a roar and everyone going every direction at once.

Daniel hasn't let go of my hand, so when he stands, I stand, too. His head swivels back and forth, and for a second, I think he's trying to find whoever fired. And that's when the next wave hits me: someone shot Winston. Someone, possibly someone nearby, wanted to shoot Winston Mendez, and did. I think it's silly for Daniel to be looking for this person. What's he going to do, fight them?

Daniel starts moving, though, dragging me behind him for a second until I realize he's moving and try to keep up with him.

"Wait," I said, but don't know why. The world snapped back into some semblance of reality.

As he moved, ducking around people, sometimes stopping them with a hand on their shoulder, I realized how small Daniel was. I hadn't ever thought about it at all, and suddenly all I could think about was how small his arms were. How small his hands. He was trying to move full grown adults out of the way. The funny thing is that people did move. He didn't shove, just put a hand on their elbow or shoulder, and they stopped moving to let him pass.

No one looked at us. Everyone's eyes were still on the stage. I wanted to look, too, but Daniel was moving so quickly that I had to keep my eyes on him and on my own feet just to keep from falling over.

It took a moment, but as we turned and started down the tunnel that lead back to the main floor, I realized what he's been doing. He wasn't looking for the person who shot Winston—he had been looking for the nearest clear exit. Just as we turned the corner to move down into the tunnel, I saw that there were others who were doing the same. The roar grew deafening. The tunnel concentrated it, made it feel like my skin was vibrating. There were a lot of people down on the main level already. They had the same look on their faces that Daniel did: determined.

I wanted to feel independent, to feel powerful, but in that moment, all I felt was glad that someone, anyone, was making decisions. Whatever this was that Daniel and I had together, it doubled as he wove in and out of the crowd, keeping me just behind him. All I could see, time and time again, was his small hand guiding people away from us. Eventually, we reached a door, and he shouldered into it. I remembered there being security guards out here, but the ramp leading to the door from the parking lot was now empty. For some reason, I wanted to zip my jacket up, but the air outside was oppressive, and I didn't want to let go of Daniel. The sudden shift from the roar to the absolute quiet that falls at around freezing left my ears ringing. Daniel's mouth was moving, but I couldn't hear what was coming out, I could only see the steam escaping.

"D-29, D-29," I finally heard.

"What?" I asked.

"Car," he said, "D-29, D-29."

I looked up to see that we were at the end of row C, and the next row had a sign saying, "D 1-30." He turned a sharp right and we moved quickly to the next to last spot. He let go of my hand, and the cold air swept over it fast. I almost protested, but he put his hand on my shoulder and guided me to the door. He quickly unlocked it, and gently nudged me inside. In one motion he pushed on my knee to get it inside the car while closing the car door.

In the absolute quiet of the car, as I waited for him to get in the driver's side, which seemed to stretch on and on, the thought occurred to me again: someone has assassinated Winston Mendez. Since when does that happen in real life?

He knocked on the driver's side door, and I turned my head, staring at him. He knocked again, and I finally get what he wants. I lean over and unlock his door. He gets in and slides the key into the ignition. The clutch squeaks. He turns the key and the little engine sputters to life.

"Seatbelt," he said.

I just stare at him.

"Seatbelt," he said, sliding his own on.

I reach over and pull mine. It takes three tries to get it into the groove. By then, he'd slid the car into reverse, and we were moving backward. Red lights come on all across the parking lot. It looked like a Christmas tree toppled on its side. First gear grinds, but gives in easily, and we moved forward.

We pull up to the toll booth under a huge sign that says "EXIT." The clutch squeaked again, and he pulled the car out of gear. We stopped, and he rolled down the window. "Already over?" the old man inside asked, "$4.50" Lights in the rearview from other cars behind us. I wonder how the old man can be so calm. I wanted to ask him, but then I it hit me: he didn't know yet. He wasn't security, and likely didn't have a radio to the inside. He didn't know, yet, what's happened. I wanted to tell him.

Daniel didn't say anything, just pulled a five dollar bill from under the visor. "Here you go; you boys have a good night." I began to lean over to tell the old man that someone has shot Winston Mendez, but then stop. What word would I use? Shot? Assassinate?

Squeak, sputter, and we moved forward, again.

We're were almost to the on-ramp, three lights down from the convention center, before there was any more noise. At that time of night, no one is downtown. Or, at least, most of those who would have been are where we just came from. I looked over at Daniel for the first time in a while, and he was rigidly staring straight ahead.

"Hey," I said. For a second, I think maybe too softly because he doesn't look. Then I touch his elbow as the light turned green, and the clutch squeaks. He looked my direction. His eyes were huge, empty. There are fifty things I think I should have said, knowing what I know now, that I wanted to say, but none of them came to mind just then. He blinked, then looked back at the road.

"They—," he started to say, but then stopped. As soon as he finished upshifting and merging, and we're on the freeway, he pressed a button on the steering wheel and said, "Call Home." The phone rang over the speakers for a few moments, then the phone picks up.

"Hello?" a woman's voice said, and I realize that I've never really heard his mom talk.

"Hi, mom?"

"Daniel? Is that you?" she asked.

"Yeah, it's me. I'm okay. I'm calling from the car and I can't talk long because we're about to get on the interstate, but any minute on the news, you're going to hear about something terrible that has happened and…and I just wanted to let you know I'm okay, and I'm coming home."

"Are you alright?" she whispered. Just in the background, I can hear the sound of a television clicking on.

"Yeah. I'm okay. I have to go, but I'll be home in a minute," he said, then clicked the button off. The speakers go dead. "If I let her say anything else it'll turn into this whole thing and I…I…" He started crying. I took his hand and held it in my lap.

I know I should call home, just like him, but what would I say?

VIKTOR

The plan was relatively simple.

They tend to be.

The people above us, whoever they are, they know that there's always the chance someone could screw up their part. So the plans stay simple. Each group has its one little part to take care of.

Things only got more complex, though, as time went on. Complex means dead.

The bullets stop for a moment. The smell of burnt gunpowder and ozone fills the room. I look around for some way out, but there isn't one.

This is the room in which I will die. A broken-down abandoned room in an unused building that no one gives a shit about. This is where.

"If you come out now, with your hands up, no weapons, I promise you that you will not be harmed."

I consider this for a moment, even though my training tells me this is a ploy. They want to take me alive so they can get answers, but also, they need time to reload. To call in backup. Right now, one of the cops is speaking into the microphone at his shoulder to another person in a room thirty miles away. That person picks up a phone and rings to another person in a room a hundred miles away. That person clicks to a second line and talks to someone else for thirty seconds, and then says "approved" when they click back over. Miles and miles above me, a satellite moves its lens to get a better look at this building and, in turn, me. It sends that information back to the second person, who then pipes it to the first and just like that, I am a known quantity. Just outside, in the hallway, one of the cops now sees a little shape of reds and oranges that is me on his small computer tablet.

"I repeat, if you come out now, hands up, no weapons, you have my word that you will be taken into custody unharmed."

This means that they won't shoot me, but once I am on an unlisted flight or buried under miles of rock in some hastily thrown together prison in Poland, that's when the harm will start. They'll call it "enhanced interrogation," but it's the same torture that humans have always inflicted on one another. These are my choices. Die here or be slowly eroded and demeaned there until I wish I had died here. Even knowing this, there is still some part of me that thinks maybe life is better. Maybe to live is to have a chance to escape at some later time. This is a lie. I know this is a lie. My training reminds me this is a lie. Still, there is that small voice, and I hate it.

Hope, here, is my enemy.

Instead, I remind myself of the suicides. Of the soldiers and what they do to little boys. Of the fathers and what they do to their sons. Of the coaches and what they do to the athletes in their care. The managers and what they do to young musicians. The fire starts to burn inside me once more.

I only managed to grab two grenades as I ran.

Before the soldiers came, and everything changed, some in town said I had an arm for baseball. I never practiced…after…but even Marcus has said how good my throwing arm is.

AARON

"I'm afraid he's not going to be able to see anyone for a little while," Daniel's mom had said and closed the door. I must have stood there just staring at the peep hole for five minutes before I turned and walked away.

Daniel hadn't been on chat and hadn't answered any of my emails for a few days, so I'd finally decided to go over and knock on the front door. It was a bit of a last resort because I really didn't know his family at all. We'd been introduced those few times, but really nothing beyond that. I hadn't been invited over for dinner. There was no telling what might be going on, and I was worried he was sick or hurt, though, so I had no choice.

Even though I didn't know quite what to expect, his mother saying that was still unexpected to say the least.

Numb, I walked to the low wall we'd shared so often and slumped. I was there for quite some time before I noticed that Marcus was sitting next to me. He hadn't said anything or touched me to let me know that he was there. As if he knew what was going on, he'd simply waited for me to notice him.

"Hey," I said.

He nodded in return.

"He's grounded or something," I said. That was the only thing I could think of—that somehow, he'd done something that had crossed a line with his parents and that they'd put him on lock down for a bit. It was the only thing I could think of that was in the realm of the possible that could cause such a reaction. Looking back over it, I wish that was all it had been.

"Oh?" Marcus said and nodded again. "I wouldn't worry. It'll all work out, I'm sure."

I nodded.

"Tea?" he asked, standing.

"Okay," I said, and I followed him back to his apartment.

"Oolong," he said, setting the mug down in front of me gently.

"Hmm?" I asked.

As with all the other times before, he apartment was tidy, and that somehow made it seem both enormous and sad.

"The tea. Oolong is what it's called. This one is from Fujian province."

I brought the mug up to my lips and Marcus said, "careful." I sipped and immediately burned my tongue.

"I wouldn't worry," he said.

"Why?" I asked.

"He likely just got himself into a bit of trouble. This kind of thing happens. In the meantime, you know that he's safe at home, so nothing bad is going to happen to him. Try to relax and know that the story will unfold itself in the fullness of time," Marcus said, bringing the cup to his own lips, blowing, then sipping. I imitated him and this time the tea didn't scald me. I took in the smell and the taste and could actually feel the warmth spreading through me.

"Yeah," was all I could think to say, though I was aware it was a stupid, childish response to what was going on.

Marcus smiled.

After a few moments, I said, "Tea is really your thing, huh?"

He set his mug down, and said, "because it doesn't just happen, like some crops. It has to be protected, molded, cultivated. Tea is like a person—it has to be grown right, then prepared correctly before it shows you what it's had inside of it."

"But don't you ever, I don't know, want a coke or something?"

He smiled, "I will make do with whatever is around me, but when I have my choice, it's tea. Do you like it?"

Before I could say anything there was a knock at the sliding glass door leading to the back yard. Something flashed across his face before it settled back down.

"Excuse me," he said and walked to the door.

He barely opened it and I couldn't see the person he was talking to, but I did hear snippets of their conversation.

"Yes?" Marcus asked.

The other man spoke quietly and quickly, but in some other language I didn't know. Some part of me thought it might be Russian because it sounded like things I'd heard in movies and on TV, but I couldn't put much trust in that.

"Good. Next step," Marcus said.

The other man again spoke quietly and quickly, but then was gone. Marcus closed the door and came back to the counter.

"Neighbors," he said. Something in his tone said I shouldn't ask more, so I didn't.

VIKTOR

The countdown is running in my head. I don't have long before they'll storm my position. The clicking sounds of them reloading stopped a while ago. I can't get my head to clear, though. It just keeps running back to all the moments that lead me here.

Marcus rolled over toward me after we're done and said, "It almost seems a shame."

"What does?" I asked.

"That we lose so many of the young ones." From completely warm and relaxed, my skin prickles. I know what he's talking about. I know who.

"That is the cause. They are heroes."

"I know," he said, nuzzling against me, "it has just always seemed a shame. Do you remember Roberto?" A backpack full of blasting gel on a subway a year and a half earlier. His dark black hair blowing in the wind on the plaza as he descended the steps without looking back at us.

"I do," I said, "but that is the way. We don't decide the missions, and we don't decide who goes on them. That's not our purpose."

He shifted up onto his elbow, "You're saying that as if you don't think I know it. I've had to recruit before."

I didn't say anything. Later, when Richard is trying to get me see his side, this is the conversation I'm thinking of.

"I wasn't trying to say anything, I was simply saying," he says, lying back down. His hand snakes out through the darkness and takes mine. I want to relax into him like before, content with the knowledge that this is all that matters—Marcus and the cause.

"New orders came in," Marcus says.

He doesn't know that I've already seen them.

"One week. A wedding," Marcus says, "Sometimes, I just wonder. If they were all still around, if the group was larger, how it might be." He goes quiet for a long time, then he says, "what we could accomplish." Not long after that, his breathing goes steady.

I remember that I closed my eyes, but sleep didn't come for some time.

All of a sudden, the even the few muffled sounds that have been happening back toward the doorway end. The whole building goes quiet.

They've decided.

AARON

A week went by. Then another. No emails. No new videos on his channel. After how his mother had acted, I felt even more self-conscious about going to Daniel's apartment again. It took me almost ten minutes of standing near their front door to get up enough courage to knock.

The door opened, and it was his mother again. "Yes?"

"I would really like to talk to Daniel, just for a second? Please?"

"No, I'm afraid he can't come to the door."

"Is he okay, though? Is he sick?" I peered past her into the apartment, but the living room beyond her was dark, unused.

"He's not allowed to have any contact with anyone," she said, and shut the door.

I wish I could say that I was strong. That my first thought was, "Fuck you, lady," and that I'd begun to plot some Tom Sawyer-esque plan for busting Daniel out. What happened, though, was that I started crying. I stood there for I don't know how long, bawling, and then walked to the low wall because I couldn't think of anything else to do.

Sitting there, I kept thinking maybe he'd just decided he didn't want to talk to me anymore, and that his parents were being helpful, running interference. Maybe I'd been dumped already but was too stupid to know it.

"Still nothing?" Marcus said from behind me.

I jumped.

"Sorry. I thought you'd heard me."

"No," I said, trying to control my voice.

He put his hand on my shoulder and patted twice. I looked up and he motioned toward the door with his head. I nodded, stood, and followed him back to his apartment.

He said nothing, though, while fixing the kettle. I sat at his table, eyes fixed on nothing, waiting until he set the mug down with a solid thunk. He sat across from me, his own mug in his hands. I put my hands on the one in front of me in the same way he had his and the warmth was comforting.

"You're thinking maybe he's decided he doesn't want to be with you anymore," Marcus said without looking at me.

I nodded, trying to keep the surprise out of my eyes.

"Do you love him?" Marcus asked.

I nodded, this time our eyes meeting. He nodded and looked down into his mug.

"Do you believe that he loves you?"

"I don't know," I whispered.

"What does your gut tell you?"

"That he does."

"And what else?"

"That something is wrong. I feel like—I feel like maybe there is something really wrong."

"Then you must act on what your gut tells you," Marcus said as our eyes met again. "You must find a way to get to him."

"But how? His mom won't even let him come to the door."

"Do you know which window is his?" Marcus asked.

"I don't know about this," I said, standing barefoot near Marcus' back gate.

"The layouts are identical in these little prefab boxes, and practice ensures success. If you feel that he is in trouble, then you must try to get to him to find out what is happening. Therefore, you must learn how to make a second floor entry."

"But what if it goes wrong? What if I get caught?"

"This is why we practice, so that you don't get caught. Now, again," he said, and gestured toward the side fence.

For the last few hours, we'd been practicing how to use the bracing bar and the columns of the fence to get to the back porch overhang and then quietly to the window which I knew to be Daniel's. Each time I tried, I failed somehow before I even made it onto the overhanging roof. The bottoms of my feet were torn and my palms were bleeding. I stepped back outside the gate and closed it behind me. So far, the one thing I had managed to get right was learning how to reach through the small gap and pull the latch back on the back gate without making any noise. I did that fairly quickly, then slipped into the backyard, quietly shutting the gate behind me and catching the latch with my pinky so that it wouldn't clink. Marcus nodded from the corner of the yard.

I crouched low as he'd shown me to do and made my way along the back fence to the place where the porch ended and the fence began. Putting my hand on top of the post there, I brought my leg up slowly until my toes were on the top of the heavier plank of wood that kept the fence's two by fours stable that ran along the fence between the posts. I took a deep breath as Marcus had told me to do, then divided my weight between my left arm and my right knee, using my back to lever myself upward. At the most awkward part of the top of the arc, I slowly brought my left foot over, placing my toes on the heavy board, as well, and moving my left hand quickly to grab the edge of the overhanging roof.

This was as far as I'd gotten in all other tries. My full weight was now resting almost entirely on my toes and the grip of my left hand on the edge of the overhanging roof.

VIKTOR

When this all first started, it was almost romantic.

I know how stupid that sounds.

But it was.

When I first joined Marcus, there were just four of them. Marcus, Aviv, Anton, and Samart. Back then, Aviv was the eldest one, the one in charge. He'd sent Marcus to bring me in. Later I found out it had been Anton who had wanted me first, but Aviv knew that Anton would have to leave. That's the structure—after the major objective is completed, one is chosen to go start a new group somewhere.

None of those boys are still around anymore, though. All that is left is Marcus and me.

"Does it hurt when they go?" I asked Marcus once, while we were all piled together on the floor under one huge blanket like we used to do.

"Always," he said. And I could see that was true.

He'd explained to me all that they knew about the history of how boys like me, like Marcus, had been used and thrown away by our societies. That all we had was each other. There was this silly pop song called "Wild Boys" from the 80s he used to sing when he thought no one was listening that, when he sang it, quiet and alone like that, suddenly meant something about us, about what we were doing.

"We are all that we have, each other," Marcus said one night after I asked him to sing it to me. With his hands on my lower back and the warmth of all of us lying on each other, our breaths almost in sync with one another, those lyrics that probably seemed so trite on the radio during the day became like poetry.

I'm thinking about this as the fourth bullet passes through my leg while I dive behind a crate left near a massive column in the middle of an empty warehouse room. That's something no one ever gets to find out until it's too late—at the moment you are dying, your brain becomes clear, clearer than it ever has been before. I can see and feel everything going on in the room from the bullets leaving their barrels coming to enter me, to the held breath of some of the agents, to the surprised look one of them has that I am still up, still shooting after so many rounds have passed through me.

The room goes quiet. I quick glance over the top of the crate to see they've pulled back behind the door. The pain hasn't hit me, yet, but I know it's coming. I remember what Aviv taught me, though—no time for crying. Check clips. Assess exit possibilities. Inventory weapons. Basic care for wounds if there is time. That all goes on autopilot.

And I know, all the way through to my bones, that if they are here for me, they already have him. That all of this may have been for nothing.

Because what could possibly matter if Marcus is already dead?

MARCUS

File 2618-69370-B
Index: 11-06:41
Room 1159B
Transcript follows:

Harper: Good morning

Prisoner: Agent Harper

Harper: The others tell me that they've finished with the other course of questioning, so no more drugs. I imagine that's something of a relief.

Prisoner: It doesn't matter one way or the other.

Harper: Is that really how you feel?

Prisoner: You want me to be happy?

Harper: I'm more invested in your wellbeing than I think you imagine.
Prisoner: Do you want to fuck me, agent Harper?

Harper: What?

Prisoner: Is that what all this is? An elaborate courtship?

Harper: I'm a married man

Prisoner: Lots of married men fantasize about lots of dirty things, agent Harper. Am I one? Something you think about while you're showering in the morning before coming here? Standing there, dick in your hand, eyes squeezed closed, wondering what I can or will do that your wife won't?

Harper: That's enough.

Prisoner: Do you want to flop me onto this table right now, agent Harper? Shove yourself into me and find out what all the fuss is about? What I'm wondering is, will you take the handcuffs off? Risk it? See if maybe you can fuck me into submitting?

Harper: That's enough! If you keep this up

Prisoner: Isn't that every police-type's fantasy? To fuck their prisoner into loving submission? Aren't you thinking that if you could get inside me, I'd suddenly do anything you ask?

Harper: I'm warning you. If you continue

Prisoner: Tell me, Agent Harper, did you ever have a boy? Another man? Haven't you ever wondered what we do when we're alone with one another.

Harper: (sound of chair scraping on floor) Enough!
(sound of skin hitting skin)
(quiet for three minutes)

Prisoner: (spitting) Feel better?

Harper: We're done here for today.

AARON

The next night, things go smoothly.

I waited until I heard the downstairs TV turn off. I tried not to hold my breath as she went up the stairs, each creak telling me which step she was on. She stopped for a minute outside my door, listening, and then I heard the floor creaking as she went to her bedroom on the other side of the stairs.

The hardest part was waiting and waiting and waiting after her bedroom door closed. Marcus said that I needed to wait at least thirty minutes to make sure that she was truly asleep, but I couldn't. After only fifteen, my legs were actually started to cramp up a bit from not moving when everything in my body wanted to.

I slid into my pants slowly. Same with the shirt. Like Marcus had told me to, I picked up my shoes and carried them with me rather than putting them on. "Bare feet are better at being silent," he told me. I followed his instructions exactly about stairs and doors and was soon out of my front door. Once I checked my pocket to make sure I remembered to take my door key, which I'd already slid off of the key ring so that the other keys and my key chains didn't make any noise, I flipped the lock and closed the door behind me. On any normal day, getting clothes on and getting out the front door would have taken ten minutes. The slow methods that Marcus had taught me made it take almost twenty-five. Still, I was out of the house long after midnight and my mother was still dozing upstairs. I slid my shoes, already laced up, on while standing, and paused for a moment.

I'd never really been out this late. Maybe it was what I was doing, maybe it was just that I was still hyped up on adrenaline from all the sneaking, but the air felt different. The colors of things seemed different in this late light.

I hurried across the complex to Daniel's family's apartment and waited. Marcus said to remember that I had to take a moment and really look at the place while my system calmed down. "Your eyes will lie to you if you let them, and with your heart thudding away, they will try. So, take a moment and breathe deep. Really look at what you're trying to see," Marcus told me. Sitting behind one apartment's air conditioner, I closed my eyes and breathed in deeply, held it, then exhaled from my stomach. I did that twice more, then opened my eyes and waited.

There were no lights on at Daniel's.

I crouch walked to the side of their backyard fence. I looked through the slats. No one was out back. Marcus had warned me to look out for this. "Sometimes, people just like to sit in darkness. Take a second, look through the slats, make sure no one is sitting on the back porch." I did as he told me in order to lift the backyard gate latch quietly, too, and in a few more moments, I was standing in front of their back porch. The smell of dryer sheets was heavy in the air.

Now or never. "Don't stay in any one place too long. You'll lose your nerve," Marcus told me, "keep moving forward so that there's not time to talk yourself out of whatever you have to do." I toed out of my shoes again, and hoisted myself up onto the fence. For some reason, the splinters and rough edges hurt more than they had at Marcus'. I was up on the overhang roof and then to Daniel's window faster than I thought I'd be.

Inside, I could see him in his bed. He was the only one of the children who got his own room, so there was no worry about any of the other kids waking up. We hadn't known each other all that long, but just seeing him made me remember all the ways we'd touched and felt.

The rough patch on the back of his left foot. The smooth skin in the crook of his elbow. The funny way his collarbones angled down instead of went straight across. For just a second, I was tempted to leave him alone. But I'd come so far.

"Just a fingernail," Marcus had warned me. "A full finger on glass would create a low note that might carry, even through cheap drywall." After the third tap, I saw Daniel's eyes open. I watched him come to the realization that someone was at his window. I saw him work through the possibilities of what he might do. Then he craned his head forward and saw that it was me. He sat up, rubbed his eyes, and then knelt at the window, sliding it open.

"What are you doing?" he asked.

"They won't let me see you," I whispered.

"I know," he said.

"Why?" I asked.

He looked behind him to make sure the door was closed. His smell came through the window and I wanted to pull him close, to have that smell and his skin close to me. He turned his head back toward me, but looked at the floor. "The thing really freaked them out. Like more than they've ever freaked out about anything. Ever," he whispered.

"Okay," I said, looking behind me to make sure no lights had come on in apartments nearby. "Keep your head on a swivel," Marcus had told me, "no matter how wrapped up in conversation you get. The longer you sit there talking, the more vulnerable you'll be, so keep your head moving to make sure you're not seen."

He put his right hand up under his shirt to hold on to his left rib-cage, a habit that always made my heart melt. "I mean, they really lost it. Everything—," he started, then stopped. "Everything has changed. It's like...like they've actually had a problem with me being gay and being out and everything, but they were hiding it from me." He leaned his forehead against the screen.

"Oh," I said. I wanted to lean my head against the screen, too, so that our foreheads touched.

"They made me delete my channel. I mean stood there over me while I did it and then checked after. They took the computer, my music...and you," he said, finally looking at me.

"What does that mean?" I whispered back.

"I can't ever see you again. At least, not while I live here."

"We'll run away, then," I whispered.

He shook his head and closed his eyes. "We're too young, Aaron. We'd never make it." That's when I finally heard it in his voice, even though it had been there the whole time.

"This doesn't make any sense," I said. I wanted him to agree with me. I wanted him to start yelling. I wanted something. Instead all he did was stare at me.

"This doesn't make any sense. It's like you're talking about completely different people. They can't have changed this much, it just wouldn't make any sense," I whispered.

He didn't say anything.

"How can they have changed this much?" I asked.

He shrugged. It infuriated me—I wanted him to fight, or at least to be mad. Instead, he just seemed deflated, like he'd already given up.

"Are you going to fight them? Fight it?" I asked.

"I yelled and I yelled and I begged and I pleaded. They won't change their minds."

"Then come away. Come with me. Right now."

His eyes fell away from mine.

"You're not going to fight it," I said, my voice slipping into regular tones.

He looked at me for a moment, then shook his head and looked away."You should have heard the things the deacon said that they agreed with. What they said to me after. If they had been yelling, I could have taken it. They were so calm. They love me, they said, and they always will, but they…they don't like this part of me. I guess they never did," he said, looking at the floor.

"Please, Daniel," I said. I don't know what I was begging him to do, but I couldn't take this.

"They're going to send me away for the rest of the summer."

"Where?" I asked, alarmed.

"This camp. It's a place where they help you not be gay."

I rocked back on my heels, almost losing balance.

"They…they really freaked out," he said, his voice wavering, "about the whole thing. They said things," even through the screen, I could see the tears well up in his eyes. "I thought," his breath caught, "I thought it was all okay this whole time, that everything was all okay, but they…"

"Come with me. Right now. Tonight. We'll get away," I said, already planning our quick run to Marcus' house and asking for his help to get away.

He looked at me for a moment as if considering it, then, just as he was about to say something, a light came on under his door. He couldn't see it because it was behind him, but I saw it.

"Light," I whispered.

He looked behind him, then slid the window closed. He whispered, "Go. Hurry. I'm sorry," as he did.

I wanted to stay rooted to that spot. I wanted to come in the window and fight for him. If this was a movie, or a novel, I might have. I might have. But because it was real life, and I was just some kid, I slid off the roof as quickly as I could. I jumped from the fence to the ground, remembering to bend my knees much further than I thought I had to so that they absorbed the sound. I grabbed my shoes and hurried out the back gate, shutting it first fast, then extremely slowly to avoid the latch making any sound.

As I snuck away behind cars, trying not to cry out at the sharp gravel cutting into my feet as I toed into my right shoe, then left, I looked back. The light was on in his room. I looked up just in time to see his mother close the blinds. I could see she was yelling.

Once I was far enough away, I walked rather than sneaking. I found myself at our low wall. Even though it was late, and I needed to get back to my house, I sat down and stared at the street lights on the highway beyond.

"So?" Marcus asked from next to me.

I jumped, but settled as soon as I realized who it was.

"He, umm...he..." and then I broke down. I leaned against him and he put his arm around my shoulder.

"Look," Marcus said after I'd cried myself out, "maybe this is just temporary. Maybe they'll come to their senses, yeah?"

I nodded against his chest.

"Here," he said, moving his shoulder a bit. I looked up at him. He used his thumb to wipe the tears away from around my eyes. "There, now."

I leaned back and he moved his arm.

"A friend of mine went through something similar," Marcus said, "people got a hold of him and took him away from me. I had no power to do anything about helping him, so all I could do was work on myself, on the world. So that's what I did," he said, nudging me a bit with his shoulder, "and that's what you'll do."

"What?" I asked, surprised at how shaky my voice was. I wiped at my eyes with the heel of my hand.

"Work on yourself. Work on changing the world. Help him by trying to make things better around him if you can't actually make things better for him."

"How?" I asked. What he proposed seemed too big, too scary.

He put his hand on my shoulder. It felt good to have someone touching me, and his hand was so big and solid that it really did steady me. "Don't worry, we'll figure something out, you and me. Right now, though, you need to get home. If your mom discovers that you're out, she might ground you, too, and then where will we be?" At the time, I thought I knew what "we" he meant, but only later did it occur to me he actually meant something else.

I nodded and stood. He pulled me into a hug. It felt so nice to have someone who understood, someone who knew it all and cared what happened that it was hard to let go for a moment. When I did pull away, he held on to my shoulders, and then walked me most of the way back to my apartment. I took off my shoes and did the same thing I'd done at Daniel's house, only this time the screen was off, and the window was open. I climbed in and shut the window behind me, then stood a moment in the dark, listening. My heart was pounding so that I was sure she'd hear it. That any moment she'd come charging through the door and start screaming.

That didn't happen, though. Eventually it was clear she hadn't woken, and so I slid out of my clothes and then sat on the edge of the bed. Thinking about the idea of somehow changing the world made me feel small again, and I looked around my room. From somewhere I didn't understand at the time, a part of me thought, "still just a boy." Now, though, I think I understand—I was already feeling what would become so clear soon.

This was the end of my childhood.

"Aaron," my mom called from downstairs, "groceries."

It occurred to me when she said it how long I'd been lying there looking at the ceiling without moving. My joints creaked as I sat up and then stood.

"Are you okay, honey?" she asked as I sat on the bottom step sliding my shoes on.

I nodded. I could tell she wanted to ask more, but stopped herself. I knew she could tell that things had changed, that something was off, but how could I have talked to her about any of this?

"'...and so, with the passage of this amendment to the constitution, marriage has been made safe from the homosexual agenda' said the senator from North Carolina. Again, the Marriage Protection amendment has been passed by a wide majority in both House and Senate, and President Thompson is expected to sign the bill within the hour. Jim, what's your take on..." the radio droned on. I stared out the window. If I had understood irony better at the time, I would have said it was ironic that at that very moment a car in front of us at the stoplight had a bumper sticker that said "It's Adam and Eve not Adam and Steve!" on the rear window. It wasn't, though, because so many cars carried bumper stickers like that these days. Little messages of hate to remind everyone that straight people were "normal" and anyone who didn't agree was clearly in the wrong.

I thought about Marcus.

"...and I think that this is only the first step to really putting an end, once and for all, to the gay agenda. I mean, look, I don't have anything against them personally. I just want them to understand that they need to keep what they do private. I mean, I don't go around demanding that everyone look at me and my wife making out in a parade—

"Yeah, Jim, but I've seen your wife, and well..."

"Is it okay if I change the channel?"

"Huh?" Mom asked. "Oh, yeah. Sure. I wasn't paying it any attention."

The next station: "...and that's got to be where it stops. Thank God almighty for some of our representatives turning back those nasty homosexuals and their gay agenda..."

The next station: "...which brings us to number one on our countdown, a new band out of Alabama called Grace, and their smash hit, 'In Jesus' Name'..."

The next station: "...and it is this same Liberal bias that keeps most news broadcasters from saying what they really mean, Jim, and that's that they don't want to talk to these baby-killing pedophile so-called authors any more than we do, but they have to because..."

I clicked off the radio.

"What if I was gay?' I asked before I knew what I was doing.

"What, honey?" Mom said, turning the radio down.

"I don't know. Never mind," I said.

"No, you asked me something. What was it?"

"I don't know. Like. What if I was gay?"

"Are you asking me if I'd still love you if you were gay?"

I didn't say anything, and I continued to look out the window.

"Are you asking because of what they're saying on the radio?"

"Do you...I dunno...do you agree with any of..?"

"No, honey, I don't. Not at all. No, what those men are saying, that's not at all how I feel. Gay people deserve just as much right to be happy as any other people. Your father and I used to talk about this a lot when we were younger, about what we'd do if you were gay. We were worried because the world was a pretty bad place for gays and lesbians and trans people even back then, and it's only gotten worse. But we knew that no matter what, we'd always love you. That's what I don't understand about so much of what people like that," she gestured to the radio, "are saying and thinking. They're assuming that just because they are the way they are that must be 'normal,' and everything that isn't how they are must not be. Which is a really stupid thing to think. Your aunt Sharon would castrate guys like that. Me, I just feel sorry for them. To have your life taken up by hate when there are so many other things to do, to feel. To be honest, I have no idea where these radio people get off, really...your job is to play music and let us know what the weather is going to be like. Just because you have a microphone doesn't mean any of us really give a shit what you think," she said and laughed. I did, too. As we pulled into the parking lot of the supermarket, she finished by saying, "but if you were to come out to me, honey, it wouldn't change a thing. Because the only thing that matters to me is that you are happy, fed, and safe. Anything else really isn't my business."

The problem was that the rest of the country, the rest of the world, wasn't thinking that way at all. The next few days, the amendment, which had been signed just a few hours after it was passed, was all anyone could talk about. I eventually stopped reading Twitter and Tumblr and all the other feeds. Out of habit, even though he'd said it was deleted, I still checked Daniel's YouTube channel to see if there were any updates, hoping maybe, maybe. The same message every time. It was gone. Deleted. No amount of wishing would bring it back.

Bit by bit, they were taking him away from me. Worse, I felt like I was letting it happen. I hadn't stormed into his house and demanded to see him. I hadn't kicked in his screen and taken him away with me. I hadn't done anything. They said, "You can't see him anymore," and I'd simply said, "Okay." I had just kept thinking it would be over soon. That they would come back to their senses and then everything would be okay again. Eventually they'd realize that they had overreacted, and everyone would take a deep breath and then he'd be here in my room again. I wanted to be with him right at that moment. I wanted to sneak out that exact second and go to his window again. It was only four in the afternoon, though. So, instead, I called Marcus.

"Can I come over?"

"Sure," he said.

MARCUS

File 2618-69370-B
Index: 12-07:57
Room 1159B
Transcript follows:

Harper: Good morning. You look terrible. Not much sleep?

Prisoner: Agent Vikram has interesting taste in music.

Harper: That he does, though I don't think he gets much choice in what they play that late at night. You could stop that from happening if you'd just cooperate.

Prisoner: He thinks I know more than I do.

Harper: When it comes to that, he and I are of the same mind.

Prisoner: And yet you two aren't communicating with one another. Do you trust him to tell you what I say?
Harper: The apartments that you and the other young

men were sharing. The landlord said that they were always paid by direct deposit on the first of the month without fail and had been for months. When we pull the bank records, though, that deposit doesn't seem to be coming from anywhere. Thoughts?

Prisoner: Are you asking me to confirm something you already suspect? That seems tedious.

Harper: And yet, I am asking.

Prisoner: For the sake of the transcript?

Harper: Let's say yes. Where were those deposits coming from?

Prisoner: I don't know.

Harper: I'm not sure I believe you.

Prisoner: We're a little far along for you to stop believing what I say, aren't we?

Harper: Your friend Viktor might disagree. I think he might urge you to rethink your cooperation level.

Prisoner: If you think that, then you don't know anything about him.

Harper: Those apartments were safehouses, weren't

they?

Prisoner: Why are you asking me to confirm or deny something which you plainly already believe?

Harper: Indulge me.

Prisoner: Why does it matter? They were apartments. We lived there for a time. We ate there, we slept there, we fucked there. What does it matter now?

Harper: Because if they were paid months in advance, then that means you and your group had a plan. A long-range plan that you carried out methodically. That will make a difference to the trial.

Prisoner: (laughter) Please tell me you're not still thinking you can fool me into trying to behave so that some judge somewhere will give me leniency. There won't be a trial. I'm not Tsarnaev or Roof. They got trials, but only because the media saw you catch them. You couldn't just make them disappear, but you would have liked that. You and agent Vikram. You'd have loved to have loaded them on a plane with no beacon and shoved them in a cell deep underneath let's see maybe Poland? It's ironic, don't you think, the way the Polish are helping you?

Harper: We're not who you think we are.

Prisoner: You don't even believe that. You already suspect what's going to happen to me once Agent Vikram gets approval from his higher-ups. If you hadn't been involved, if he'd have had the chance to question me first? I'd already be in a prison that doesn't technically exist somewhere in the world. You got here first, though, so they can't just disappear me without there being some record in the files at Quantico. As we speak, they're moving someone into position who will be able to blank the files the moment you have decided you've gotten everything you can from me. That night I will cease to exist. Do you think I don't know these things?

Harper: You have a very active imagination.

Prisoner: And you have an overactive denial mechanism.

Harper: I thought we were farther along than this.

Prisoner: You're still a straight male, agent Harper. When you leave here today, the rest of the world is bent to your every whim. We've been talking a while now, and even though you've stopped wearing your wedding ring when you come in here, there's still a tan line there. You're an outdoors type of person, so you're used to taking it on and off I imagine, but you wear it like a good little boy, so there's still some trace. You take it off before you come in to see me because you don't want me to talk about your wife. You've told her that if I start in on her, you don't know what you'll do. You're that kind of person, I can tell. You believe in bringing depraved criminals like me to justice, and this one just so happens to be a faggot, too, so you feel doubly justified.

Harper: You don't know what you're talking about.

Prisoner: Who was he, agent Harper? The first boy who noticed your powder blue eyes and dark hair? The first one who let you know that he wouldn't mind helping you relax a bit after the big game? Did you consider it? Did you even maybe let him stroke you off?

Harper: You need new material, and we're done here.

Prisoner: Are we, Agent Harper? Are we?

VIKTOR

"A word?" Richard asked me one night not long after the change in plan. It's more than a bit unusual for Richard to talk to me at all. We don't hate one another—I don't hate any of them. And I know from experience that Richard would take a bullet for me, for any of us. It's just that, as with any group, there are subgroups. Richard and I don't tend to have the same subgroup. He tends to stick with the Europeans, even though he's Irish. I've always been more comfortable with the boys who come to us from everywhere else.

I followed him without saying anything. Once we were outside and away from the others, he lit a cigarette with his hand cupping over the top of the lighter. He gestured the pack toward me, but I don't smoke. He flicked the lighter closed with one hand and pushed the pack into his breast pocket with the other.

"What is it?" I asked.

"You're getting really quite good," he said. "No trace of any accent at all. No matter how hard I try, I can't get the shamrocks out of mine, but you could be on fuckin' cable news."

"I get the feeling you don't consider that a compliment," I said.

Richard took a long drag on his cigarette and exhaled a steady stream upward. "This one feels different," he said, his eyes scanning the rooftops of the other apartments nearby.

At that moment, I was relieved and appalled at myself to feel that way. I wanted to agree with him and to take some comfort that I wasn't alone in feeling so. But that also felt like a betrayal, some kind of final act. Almost like an admission that I'd been wrong all those years ago to follow Marcus in the first place.

"I'm not saying anything against him," Richard continued without waiting, "but what I am saying is this: I've been here a while. Not as long as you, I know, but a while. I've seen a lot of these young fellas come and go. You have, too. I've never seen him act like this about any of them."

So. He was thinking the exact same thing I was. "I'm not trying to say anyone should be putting an age limit on the thing. They sure don't, for fuck's sake," he said, gesturing toward the rest of the world with his chin. "You and I know that better than anyone. I made my first bomb at eleven after they cut down little Liam right the fuck in front of me. He was only nine."

I remembered. I had only been five years older than that when I watched Itakshir, who had been in charge then, show Richard how to wire the thing.

"But this, it feels different. Less like with the rest of us. More like something else. Something I don't like," he said, and spit off of the porch. "Funny thing is, I look around and I don't see anyone else with the same feeling. Except maybe you."

"What is it you want to ask?"

"Don't give me the famous Viktor stone wall routine. I know you'd fuckin' well defend him to the devil himself, but the thing is I've seen the look you give the little fucker when the big man is doting on him. I've seen it, and I know it. So can we skip the formalities and talk like men for a moment?"

"Let's say you're right—"

"I fuckin' well am,"

"—and he is doing something different. Something more like them," I said, copying his gesture toward the rest of the world with my chin, "than what we do. So what? What's different about the outcome?"

"Only this," he said, taking a drag off the cigarette, "if he's sweet on the little fucker, if this isn't about brotherhood, then what's to say that at the last minute he doesn't try to stop what has to happen?"

And there it was. The thing I'd been dreading, too. The unwritten rule for all of us—our times together with one another were comfort for the dead, the spirit of the trenches. We weren't supposed to take lovers, we were instead comforting each other until time was up. The cause was the thing we pledged our lives to, the cause that saved us, and that welded us together heart, mind, and other places. If one of us were ever to falter when it came time to pull a trigger or press a button, that was it. It wasn't something we talked about at all, but we all knew it.

"We chose the first one because he was already fighting for the cause on the fuckin' internet. We all agreed on that one. But then this last minute shift—"

"Circumstances changed. You know that," I said.

"They did. However, where was the meeting after that to figure out what to do? The one in charge gets to make a lot of decisions by himself, I know the rules as well as you do, but let me ask you this—when was the last time one got to decide who gets brought in and who doesn't all by their lonesome?"

The door to the patio opened and Mazhar poked his head out, "He's back."

Richard took a final pull of his cigarette, dropped it on the concrete and then stamped it out. I walked toward the door, but he put his hand on my shoulder.

"You're not saying it, but I know you agree. Time's coming, though, where you're going to have to make a decision. I hope to Mary that you know what the right one is when you do." He turned and went inside.

AARON

Three more days passed. I would love to say that I pined away for Daniel, that I simply sat in my room, staring at the wall. That we lived in that kind of a fairy tale world.

I talked to my mother and tried to pretend nothing was wrong. I cooked dinner and tried to pretend nothing was wrong. I rode my bike around the surrounding few blocks and tried to pretend nothing was wrong.

I talked to Marcus, though, and I could tell him all of it. Everything.

I could only get away to his apartment for an hour or so at a time, but it was what I needed. I didn't have to pretend nothing was wrong when I was there. Over those few days, I started to meet several of his friends and roommates, which I didn't know he had. They were from all different countries, and they were all absolutely beautiful.

"This is Viktor," Marcus said on the second day. Viktor was tall, thin and cut with muscles the same way Marcus was, with wavy brown hair. He, like Marcus, also had an accent that I couldn't quite place. I didn't feel like I could ask, though.

"Hello," Viktor said, and I could feel that he didn't like me instantly.

"Viktor, this is Aaron, the boy I've been telling you about."

Viktor nodded, then went upstairs. "Excuse him," Marcus said to me, "he's a bit awkward around new people." Just then, the kettle whistled, and Marcus went to fix our tea. I was just about to follow him when Viktor came back down the stairs. He had a large bag with him, and I could see a wrapped handle poking out.

I knew I shouldn't ask, but I couldn't stop myself. "Is that a sword?"

Viktor, who had been picking up his sunglasses from the table near the door, stopped and turned toward me. He looked at the handle, then back at me, and said, "yes."

Marcus was just coming back into the room then. "Where are you off to?" he asked, smiling.

Viktor said something in a language that sounded like Russian. Marcus said something very short back, and Viktor turned and left.

"Awkward, like I said," Marcus said to me, handing me the green mug. The warmth felt good on my hands, even though it was hot outside.

"Was…was he carrying a sword?" I asked.

"Kendo. Or, at least, the closest approximation any of us can find to it, here."

"Kendo?"

"Learning to work with the sword. Like fencing in a lot of ways."

"Oh," I said, and sipped the tea.

Marcus moved to the couch and sat. I followed. "It's something we all do, my friends and I."

"Is Viktor a friend and a roommate?"

"It's fairly complicated, but yes," Marcus said. "It's an old idea," he said, and I could tell he was switching subjects, "but almost all great societies have the idea that a person has a duty to keep a sound mind in a sound body. Working out to maintain health and readiness rather than to show off for sex partners. Do you have a fitness routine of some sort?" he asked, and in his tone I could tell he knew I didn't.

"No," I said, looking away.

"Ah," he said. "You know, it would help you through what you're feeling right now."

I looked at him.

"You're anxious about your friend. He's so close but you can't contact him, and now you're worried about what his parents will do. Your body is all geared up, fight or flight systems engaged. Your brain is dumping little bits of adrenaline into your system constantly because it doesn't know the difference between what you're feeling and an actual dangerous situation. Here," he said, "stand up."

I did as he asked. He moved close to me, putting his hands on my elbows. He pushed them up, so that my hands were near my face. "Make fists," he said. I did.

He stepped back from me and adopted a similar stance.

"Hit me," he said.

"What?" I asked.

"I want you to try to hit me."

"How is this going to make me feel better?" I asked. The second I finished, he swung his fist toward my face. I barely got my own fist up in time to block it.

"Hit me," he said.

I gave a weak attempt at a jab. He pushed it away easily, then threw another punch my way. I blocked it, but I could tell he had swung harder than the first time.

"Again," he said.

"I don't want to do this," I said, lowering my fists.

He swung in and slapped my face. I was so stunned I couldn't say anything.

"Again," he said.

"No," I said, angry.

He slapped me again. Then again. The third time he tried, I got my fists up and blocked it.

"Good. Now, again," he said.

I made a half-hearted attempt at a jab. He blocked it easily and swung in, slapping my face. I was so angry that my face went hot and my throat closed up. I swung at him and he blocked it, but not as easily. He snuck in through my blocking and slapped me once more. I swung harder and actually managed to graze his chin. His next swing wasn't a slap, it was a punch.

I'd never been punched before. Some part of me watched, fascinated, while my nose began to bleed.

"Again," he said.

I swung with all the fury I felt at that moment. He blocked, but I could see in his eyes for a second that I'd surprised him. Some animal part of me liked that. I swung again, not waiting for us to take turns. He blocked and swung. I moved my fists to block and managed to stop him.

"Tuck your head in further. Think about the rabbit in its hole." I ducked further into the space between my fists, rolling my shoulders forward some.

I swung on him again, then again, and he swung again. I blocked it, but this time I could tell he was really swinging; my fist bounced off of my own face from the force of blocking him.

"Come on, you can do this. Hit me!" he yelled.

I stepped in and swung. He blocked and hit me twice in the stomach. I doubled over and went to one knee.

"Get up," he said. I looked up at him, my whole body vibrating with how angry I was. "There it is," he said, almost in a whisper. "There—do you feel that? That rage? That anger? Concentrate on it. Use it and get up."

I thought for a second that I didn't understand what he meant, but the lizard part of my brain knew. I found myself standing up, tucking back into the hole between my fists, and moving one leg forward. I knew, now, that I had to watch out for more than just my head.

"There," he said, smiling. Even though I was furious with him, that smile, that approval, meant everything to me. "Again," he said. Suddenly, he swung on me several times in a row. I managed to block and step backward, but the last blow hit hard.

We went on like that for an hour or so, then he stopped us. "Now," he said, while we both panted, "spread your legs shoulder width apart and relax your hips some." I did as he asked. "Relax your knees," he said, and I did. "Relax your shoulders," he said, and I did. "Relax your neck," he said, and I did. "Breathe in deep through your nose and hold it," he said. I did. He waited a moment then said, "exhale, pushing from your stomach out." I did. We went through the process several more times, then he said, "now, open your eyes." When I did, I found that I felt better than I had in weeks.

"Good," he said, and put his hand on my shoulder. I found myself wanting his approval in that moment. "Good. Now, go home, take a luke-warm shower—no hot water—and then lie down for a bit. No computer."

I started to protest that I wanted to stay, to talk more, but I could see in his eye that he expected me to obey immediately. So, I did.

VIKTOR

Of course, it's going to have to be me.

If it finally gets back to him and he finds out anyone else did it, he'll have to kill them. So long as it's me, there's at least a chance he won't do anything.

For a week now, I've known it was going to have to be me. Thing is, though, even with all that I've done since joining, I've never had to kill someone and make it look like a suicide. We normally want there to be a lot of noise and attention to our killings, so we tend to learn to leave signs, clues to let authorities know that it was us. We want the credit.

It just so happens that one night, when I'm on my way to the kid's window to figure out how to do it, I'm passing by the other kid, Aaron's apartment that I see him come slipping out of his front door. I slide into the shadows waiting for the kid to look around, then follow him from a distance as he starts off. There's no danger he can see me, not with it this dark out and not considering where I'm hiding. He is moving fairly boldly for someone trying to sneak, so for a second I think he might not be, but then I notice where he's heading. I positioned myself at a distance from the apartment I know he's trying for. I wonder for a second if this is an attempt to have sex. I'm watching him slip out of his shoes, muffle the sound of the back gate latch fairly well, then slip into the backyard.

It's not until I see the way he positions himself to swing up onto the roof that it hits me: those are Marcus' moves. I should know; I was there the same day. We were both trained to move like that. I watch him as he moves up the overhang to the other boy's window. I can see them talking and without being anywhere near earshot, I can tell what's happening. I don't know why, but it's clear that this is goodbye. From what I've seen of that house's habits, they don't have too much longer to talk before someone gets up to pee and hears noise. Maybe five more minutes at the outside.

The boy scrambles down the overhang and goes back through the same steps only in reverse. He's in and out in under ten minutes with no one seeing him. That's Marcus' training. That makes me even more sure. I followed him, thinking "I could do it now." Instead of taking the turn back toward his house, though, he turns the opposite way. He's heading to the low wall that borders the property. I've seen him and the other boy sit there some evenings. When he gets there, he sits down and I position myself at a distance once more. I could do it now.

Then Marcus shows up. Then Marcus sits down next to the boy. Then Marcus puts his arm around the boy. Then the boy leans his head on Marcus' shoulders.

Jealousy? Consideration for the mission? I have no idea what it was, but at that moment I felt more than ever that I had to do this.

AARON

It took two more weeks before I got up enough nerve to knock on the door again. During that time, I was with Marcus a lot. He was the only person on the planet who understood. We drank tea, he showed me things about hand-to-hand fighting and weapons, about breathing properly, he talked to me about history, the Stonewall riots, GRIDS, everything. It helped to pass the time and keep Daniel off my mind some. We spent a lot of time talking in the backyard of his apartment while he showed me forms with practice swords or with open hands and then fighting one another, which he called sparring.

But there were still the nights. As soon as I'd get home, I would eat dinner, talk with mom for a bit, go upstairs and let off some pressure, then watch episodes of Bleach until I was ready to fall asleep. I would close my laptop, shut off the bedside lamp and turn over, imagining falling slowly down a long, dark hole like Marcus had told me. But then I'd remember Daniel's face. I'd remember how soft the skin on his upper thigh was. I'd remember his laugh. Then there'd be no sleep.

After two weeks of that, I was going crazy. I know people say that a lot, but that's how it felt. Every time I thought about Daniel, it was like my stomach was spinning faster and faster but my head was staying still. My legs felt tense, like I needed to get up and run, but there was nowhere to go. Toward the end of that time, I went so far as to sneak all the way to his backyard again, and almost up to his window, but when I was just about to shift my weight up onto the fence, a light came on in the kitchen, which faced the backyard. I have no idea how the person who was in there didn't see me, but luckily enough they didn't.

"I have to go talk to them. Maybe they've calmed down," I said to Marcus.

"Maybe, but isn't likely," he said, shifting his weight so that the practice sword he was holding changed its pressure on the one I was holding, and I fell forward onto the grass.

He reached out a hand to help me up. I took it, bending at the knees.

"Maybe if I keep going over there, they'll see that I love him. That I can't be turned away."

"That's less likely. Remember, he's a child to them. He said so to you," Marcus said, putting his practice sword up at first position again. I shifted my weight onto both feet and placed my sword against his. "They reacted as though they'd made a mistake giving him freedoms, which means that" he said, moving through the first three forms. I blocked in the ways that he had taught me to, "they now see him as even more of a child than they did before." At the end of that three move run, he backed up and placed himself in first position again. I moved toward him and did the same.

"But I can't just keep doing nothing," I said. This time, as we'd done so many times before, we switched, and I made the first three moves. He blocked with the standard blocks. "Are you saying I should do nothing?"

He lowered his sword, and I immediately did the same for safety as he'd shown me. He looked at the ground, then back at me, "I'm saying that, if you go to the house again, they might see that as a last straw rather than proof of your love. Whatever you decide to do, know that this could be the end of the end rather than the beginning of a new chapter. Make peace with that."

It took me three hours of convincing myself before I could finally get up the nerve to knock. I'd been walking aimlessly around the complex that entire time because I knew if I went home, I'd talk myself out of it. If I just stayed walking, I wasn't doing nothing, but I wasn't doing the thing that made me scared, either. Finally, though, some part of me got numb enough to decide that it was now or never.

The first three knocks on their front door were so soft, I was sure no one had heard them. I made myself knock harder for the second three. The door opened, and it was Daniel's father.

"Aaron," he said, but something was wrong with his face. There was no movement of recognition or anger or anything else.

"Please let me talk to Daniel," I said. It came out far more whiny than I wanted, but there was no taking it back now.

"I'm afraid...uh...there's..." he said and immediately I knew something was horribly wrong. "Why don't you come in?" he said.

I went inside and noticed that there were no lights on. As he closed the door behind me, I jumped, because there was no sound, either. The whole house was quiet. He walked around me and then over to the sofa. He sat sideways in a way that let me know he wanted me to sit down beside him.

"Aaron, something happened," he said, and at that last word, his whole face twisted as if to shatter, but then came quickly back under control. "Something," he said, and I could hear the sob just barely held back in his voice, "Umm...something has happened. Something terrible." I waited. "We thought it would be best for Daniel to spend some time at a camp one of our Deacons told us about. They help young men find their way back to...to how things should be." Without him saying it, I knew he meant sexuality reprogramming. Marcus had told me about these camps, usually associated with churches, that kids like me and Daniel were often sent to against our will, to be taught how to be straight. Without consciously deciding to, I scooted further away from Daniel's father.

"Things seemed to be going fine for the first week, but then the counselors say he stopped trying. That he almost seemed to want to be punished he was acting out so willfully. They...umm...they were just about to call us to come talk to him when he...uh...Daniel, he..." and at that point, Daniel's father broke down. I've never seen a grown man cry before except in movies and even though I was angry at him, I felt some desire to comfort him, too. Instead, I didn't move. Daniel's father cried like that for a few minutes, his sobs the only sound in the house except for the ticking of an old clock in the hallway.

He eventually calmed down, getting control of his breathing. "Uh," he said, wiping his face with the palm of his hand, "Aaron, Daniel took his own life a few days ago at the camp."

I don't know how long I sat there without saying anything, without moving, waiting for him to say that he was joking or that say something else to clear up what couldn't have been what he meant, but nothing happened. The quiet was all.

"I don't understand," I said.

"Daniel committed suicide a few days ago. He's...umm...he's gone," Daniel's father said, looking at the wall behind me the whole time.

"I don't understand," I said.

"We didn't know," he said, breaking down again. "We didn't know." He leaned in toward me as if for a hug, but I stood up and backed away.

"You're lying!" I said and ran down the hall and up the stairs. "You're lying to me! Daniel!" I yelled.

"Please," Daniel's father said, following me slowly.

At the top of the stairs, I saw that all of the bedrooms were open, all of the beds made, nothing on the floor, but no one else was here. I went into Daniel's bedroom. It was tidy in a way that he'd said it never was.

His old computer was on the desktop. I don't know why, but I went to it and put my hand on top of the tower. It was cold. For some reason, that cold seeping through my palm into me convinced me it was final.

"Please," Daniel's father said, stumbling slowly into the room. He'd yet to finish the sentence, but it didn't matter.

I turned to him, my hand still on the cold computer. I wanted to curse him, I wanted to say something so perfectly vicious that he'd never recover. I wanted to let him know that it should be him that was dead. Instead, I said nothing, staring blankly. Tears ran down his cheeks while he stood there, staring back at me.

I kept thinking that I was about to feel something. That I was about to scream. Nothing came, though. After a long moment, I walked past Daniel's father down the stairs and out the front door.

Without willing it, I found myself at Marcus' door.

"He's dead," I said and I honestly couldn't tell you what happened after that for a while.

"Aaron," Marcus said. I knew he was up there, somewhere, but down here there was darkness and warmth and for once the bones in my legs didn't ache. "Aaron, I can tell that you heard me. Wake up," Marcus said, his voice soft. I felt his hand on my shoulder. I knew I should wake up to find out where I was, what was going on, but I also knew that right behind Marcus, right there beside him, was something else. Something huge and frightening. To wake up was to invite it to attack me.

"Is he going back to his parents or is it time?" someone else said. Dimly, I remembered the name started with V, but not the rest of it.

"It's not time just yet. Soon, but not now." I drifted back down into darkness.

Later, when my eyes opened by themselves, it was dark in the room. I didn't recognize any of the furniture, but the smell of green tea was in the air. A mug sat on a coffee table nearby. Across the table in another chair was Marcus. I pushed up onto one elbow and saw that we were in his living room. It was night outside the windows.

"You're safe," he said without moving. In the darkness, his voice seemed bigger than it had in the past.

"How…?" I started but trailed off.

"You came to my door. You were howling and sobbing. I took you in before someone came to investigate." Something in my mind wanted to turn over that choice of words a bit because it seemed somewhat odd, but it was at that moment that it all came rushing back to me, and my throat closed up. "From what I've been able to piece together while we got you calmed down, something terrible has happened to Daniel. Is that correct?" Again, something in his word choice tickled at the back of my brain. It was as if he was somehow a different person than the one that Daniel and I had met.

I couldn't say it. I couldn't say anything. I nodded, even though it was dark in the room. He must have understood, though, because he said, "I see. Was it something that was done to him, or something that he did to himself?" Something in his voice was tight, controlled. Dangerous. I could tell that how I answered would determine something very important.

I sat up, noting that I was mostly undressed as the blanket fell away from me. Oddly, even though it was dark in the room, and I did still have on underwear, I felt like Marcus could see all of me. I pulled the blanket up around my shoulders.

"He…umm…he…his father said that…that while he was at the camp they sent him to…that he…umm…that he committed suicide while he was there." Some part of me, outside of myself, was amazed that I'd said it without breaking down.

"I see," Marcus said. The silence that descended was total, as if somehow he'd managed to muffle the outside world simply by willing it. "There's tea," he said without gesturing. The part of me that was outside, watching, noted that I picked up the mug and sipped not because I was thirsty, but because it was something he wanted me to do. I agreed with it.

"I have to talk to Viktor. You can stay here."

"I should maybe call my mom," I said, surprised by how calmly.

He stood without saying anything and laid my phone on the coffee table, then walked out the sliding glass door, closed it behind him, and then walked out the back gate. I leaned over and turned on the lamp next to the couch. My clothes were folded neatly on the floor nearby. I considered not getting into them. Some part of me felt that, if I got off this couch, out from under this blanket, that if I put my clothes on, I would be part of the world, again, and I'd then have to think about what had happened. I'd have to deal with the fact that Daniel was gone. That I hadn't even gotten to say goodbye. It was the same with the phone. I knew I needed to call my mom—it was darker outside the windows than it normally would have been for me to come wandering home. I knew that, by now, she would be worrying. But if I picked up the phone, if I heard the phone ringing on the other end, then I was a part of the world, again, and that meant dealing with it.

So, I sat there, staring at the phone for what seemed like hours. Then I picked it up and pressed 1. She picked up almost immediately.

"Aaron Lee Miller, where are you?"

"I'm sorry. I lost track of time. I'll be home."

"Now, young man."

"Okay," and I hung up. Putting the first sock on took forever and my shoulders got heavier and heavier. Even though it seemed to take a long time, though, I was fully dressed before Marcus made it back. I needed to get home, but I didn't want to leave his house unlocked. I stood there in his empty apartment for a while, perfectly still, waiting. After fifteen minutes, I knew I had to leave, and I hoped he'd forgive me for leaving it unlocked. Just as I closed his sliding glass door behind me, I turned and he was there.

"I need to go," I said. He stepped aside without saying anything. "Thank you," I fumbled past him, "for...you know...I...thanks."

"We should talk," he said, "tomorrow."

"Okay," I said, and walked home.

I knew she would have questions.

I didn't know how I was going to answer them.

MARCUS

File 2618-69370-B
Index: 13-09:15
Room 1159B
Transcript follows:

Harper: Good morning.

Prisoner: Tell me about Viktor.

Harper: From what I've been told, he's doing well. Not conscious, yet, but stabilized. That's all I know, but if anything changes, they know to call me.

Prisoner: He's strong.

Harper: Why don't you tell me more about him, about how you recruited him, or the others?

Prisoner: That's not how the setup works.

Harper: Then tell me about how it works.

Prisoner: We don't get to decide. That's all taken care of higher up.

Harper: By who?

Prisoner: I don't know.

Harper: But you have some guesses. I can tell.

Prisoner: I don't.
(silence for a one minute)

Harper: When the word comes down from on high who to recruit, then, do you get a say? Could you have said no to the order to bring Aaron Miller in?

Prisoner: No.

Harper: And you still maintain that Aaron Miller wasn't your decision? That someone else just happened to want this kid who just happened to be living in the same apartment complex as the safehouses that were established for you before you even arrived for the Mendez job?

Prisoner: Yes.

Harper: That seems like an awful lot of coincidence.

Prisoner: The world is a funny old place, isn't it?

Harper: Look, I can help. That Vikram and his goons

are going to disappear you isn't a done deal. If you tell me what I want to know, I can help you. You'll never be free again, but at least you won't be God knows where. There's a chance you might even be able to see Viktor again.

Prisoner: Don't try to play mind games with me, Agent Harper. You and I both know that no matter how hard you try, I will be three stories below ground in some off the books site in Poland by next week.

Harper: What makes you think that's inevitable?

Prisoner: Because if there's even a chance someone might find me, then there's a chance my story might get out. That somehow, somewhere, some other gay person might decide that they want their rights and that they would be willing to stand up for them with arms, if necessary. Your government can't take that chance. Not with the other plans in the works.

Harper: You keep talking about all these crazy conspiracy theories as if they are proven fact. You have to see that's not helping your case.

Prisoner: Or is it you who is crazy for not seeing that your straight, white, male government will stop short of nothing to roll the clock back to the time when they thought that they were in full control? Hence black site prisons here on our own soil. Hence the leap in genetic coding research. Find the "gay gene" and turn it off for the children not yet born, round up and exterminate all the gays already walking around. The plans are already on the books, Agent Harper. I would imagine that a date has already been set.

Harper: You sound like a broken record. On and on and on about all of this. How does any of what you're doing right now help Viktor? Last chance for today tell me about your recruitment practices.

Prisoner: Do you think there's any chance that, if he does wake up, he won't go out and find a way to start it all up again? Do you think I don't know you've already thought of that? Do you think that I truly believe you'll let him live?

Harper: We're nowhere, today. We're done, here.

AARON

The next day Mom didn't make a fuss and wake me up. Being awake was like the surface of the ocean. I sat beneath, looking up, considering what the world was like up there, but I refused to come up. I was no longer dreaming, but I refused to open my eyes.

She had asked me questions but before I could answer, I broke down crying. She kept trying to get more answers, thinking that I would be able to get control, but I didn't. I didn't want to get control. Once she realized that, the questions stopped, she took me into her arms and let me cry. I fell asleep that way, and it felt like falling, endlessly falling into a deep black trench.

Because of that, I had no idea how long she'd been gone before I heard Marcus' voice. "Aaron," he said. I had the feeling it wasn't the first time he'd called my name, but that name, and Marcus, were all a part of the world up above. They could stay there; I'd remain down here.

"Aaron, get up," Marcus said. The amount of light on my eyelids changed. I felt a hand move through my hair.

When I opened my eyes, Marcus was standing in my living room. When I fell asleep on the couch, Mom had simply covered me up and left me there.

"The funeral is today. We need to go."

I closed my eyes again and reached for the blanket which he'd folded back. He held onto it. "No. This is important. Get up." He pulled it down even further so that the warmth it had held dissipated quickly.

"How did you get in?" I asked without opening my eyes.

"Does that matter? Get up or we'll be late." He put his hand on my upper arm and pulled it slowly toward him. My choice was to follow it or to wind up uncomfortable. At no point was he hurting me, but it was clear that I wasn't going to be able to remain in bed. It was only then that what he had been saying all along occurred to me.

Today, the Youngs were burying Daniel. Somehow, I hadn't even though to ask if there was going to be a funeral or when it was. I opened my eyes and sat up. His hand was still on my arm, which he put a bit more pressure on. "Here," he said, pressing a pile of clothes into my arms and moving a step back so that I had to move my feet from the bed to the floor. I took the clothes and stood up.

"How did you get in?" I said and he then moved me one step at a time toward the bathroom where the shower was already running.

"There isn't much time. Get dressed." With that, he released my arm in a way that still moved me a step or two forward as if pushed. I showered and got dressed, half expecting him to come upstairs while I did, but when I came back down, he was standing with the front door open.

As I picked up my keys and put them in my pocket, I saw the calendar that mom kept pinned up near the front door. She crossed off each day the following morning so that the past was a series of slashes and the future was clear. I saw the date: summer break was almost over.

"How will we even know which one it is?" I asked.

"It's the only one in that cemetery today," Marcus said.

Viktor in his dark sunglasses drove the beat-up old Toyota with Marcus in the front seat and me in the back. None of us said anything. The only sound was the whining of the gears as they struggled to keep up with Viktor's aggressive driving. As soon as we pulled through the gate and wound around the tiny roads, Marcus put on his own glasses, and handed a pair to me. We all got out and walked across several other plots until we arrived at the back of the group.

The preacher or priest or deacon or whatever you call them was already into his talk. "And though he was a confused young man, so angry and full of doubt, toward the end he began to find his way thanks to the helpful volunteers and staff at The Retreat. Though none of them could be here today, we want to thank them for attempting to show young Daniel a better way, a cleaner way, shining with the light of the Lord. Today, we will remember not only who Daniel was, but that he was working toward his salvation at the end. He had turned away from the wickedness of his fornication and lust and toward the peace and everlasting light of Jesus," the man was saying.

Almost too low to hear, Viktor said to Marcus, "I thought the boy was Mormon."

Marcus whispered back something, the only word I caught was "conversion."

From our place in the back, I couldn't see Daniel's family, but I knew they were up there, on the front row. The image of them agreeing with what this man, who didn't know Daniel at all, was saying made me mad. My hands clenched into fists.

"Daniel was a creative soul, possessed with a singular drive to put himself into the world through the miracle of the Internet. Of course, the message he spread in those videos was misguided and vile, but we want to celebrate his ingenuity, not condemn his mistakes. We can only guess at what he might have been able to do if he had been speaking righteousness and spreading The Good News. This is what makes his passing so sad—that there was so much potential for good in him. That he was on his way to better things," Both my hands were clenched into fists and my breathing had sped up. My heart was thundering through my chest; I felt as though everyone could hear it. That any moment, they'd turn around to find out what that sound was. Worse, I could see them all nodding along with what this man was saying. I wanted to scream. I wanted to start punching them. My fists were coming up toward my chest when Marcus put a hand on my shoulder. I looked at him, seeing my face reflected in his glasses. He shook he head and gave the most gentle nudge back toward the car. Viktor was already moving that way.

I looked back toward the grave, at least what I could see of it from where I stood, and then turned to follow Viktor. Marcus walked behind. The sound of the priest or preacher or whoever faded slowly, but I didn't have to hear him anymore to know what he was doing.

We drove all the way back to Marcus' apartment without saying anything to one another.

The tea Marcus sat before me smelled incredible. Viktor took his from Marcus' hand before he could set it down. Marcus then set his own mug down and slid into the chair on my right side.

"So," Marcus said. "The camp was called The Retreat. It was in Puerto Rico," he said, handing me a pamphlet. I didn't touch it. "It's a Christian organization designed to reprogram what they call, 'wayward youth.' To bring them back to what they call Christ's teachings. Because it's in a territory and not a state, there are differences in the regulations, differences places like this," he said, tapping the pamphlet twice, "and there are many, exploit."

Viktor was the last to take his sunglasses off. He slid them into the pocket inside his coat. None of us said anything for a moment.

"I wanted you to see," Marcus said. "This is what they think of us. They despise us enough to turn a boy's funeral into a hate rant."

"Us?" I asked, looking at Viktor.

"Gay people. They hate us," Marcus said, gesturing toward Viktor then me. "They want us all in that grave."

"You're…?" I asked, looking at Viktor.

"We all are. All of my group," Marcus said.

"Group?"

Marcus picked up his mug, and, sipping from it, leaned back in his chair.

Viktor looked from me to Marcus, "Are you sure?"

"Yes," Marcus said.

Viktor got up and walked out the sliding glass door and then the back gate.

"After everything I've told you, can you see that we are not some anomaly? That we are not merely a subset of them?" he said, gesturing toward the window with his chin. "We are our own culture. We are our own species."

"I'm not sure I understand…" I said.

"Things are moving very fast, I understand that. I do. But on some level, you have to have felt it. How much they hate us. You have to have wondered why that is. What could cause that. It's more than just their discomfort because of a stupid book. There has to be more to it." He moved forward until he was barely in his chair. Our knees were nearly touching, and his hand was on my shoulder. "Aaron, they know that we are our own society. They can sense that gay people don't need their rules, their morality. We have our own. And it scares them to think that they have so little control over us. That we need nothing from them. Not their culture, not their laws, and certainly not their approval."

Just then Viktor came back in from outside with several other young men and boys with him. The room was suddenly crowded. They were black, white, Asian, short, tall, skinny, bulky, with green eyes and black eyes and crystalline blue eyes, blonde, brunette, redheaded with shaved heads and close-cropped afros and ponytails. I was overwhelmed. Once one of them near the back had closed the sliding glass door, Marcus continued, "This is my group. Everyone, this is Aaron." There were some hellos, and greetings in many other languages, as well.

I remembered earlier how I had paid attention to when people moved in and when they moved out. I'd known when someone was new. It was only at that moment that I knew I'd seen these boys and young men around, but paid no mind to it. I'd been so wrapped up in Daniel that I hadn't asked myself or anyone else who these guys were, where they lived. They'd been here, but only now did I truly see them.

"Hello," I said, my social programming kicking in on autopilot.

"Aaron," Marcus said, "What they've done to you, what they've taken from you, can never be replaced." He stood, taking a few steps back so that he was the focus of everyone's attention. "Aaron has had something taken from him. Something precious. He had just begun to feel love when the straight agenda moved to crush that beautiful moment," as he spoke, I could see the faces of those who had come in grow dark, fill with anger. "They shipped a young boy off to be reprogrammed at one of their death camps, congratulating themselves on doing what their church wanted. There, alone, in the dark, hurting, that young man took his own life." Many of those in the room started to murmur. More than one had tears in their eyes. "They took this young boy from the comfort, the solace, the love that Aaron was ready to give without so much as a thought for their own son's safety, let alone what Aaron is now left to feel." The sadness that many were expressing was coupled with anger.

Marcus fell quiet for a moment. A few of them put hands on each other's shoulders or around each other's waists. Two of them who were standing behind the couch put their hands on my shoulders. "As some of you know already, we came here for a purpose. One of our tasks is already complete, but the second task waits. Before we decide who will take on that glorious burden, I propose something. Something perhaps radical, maybe too different, too sudden," he said, and fell quiet, looking at the floor.

"What is it?" one of the young boys asked. Several others chimed in asking him to tell them.

"No, it's too much. I can't ask it of you," Marcus said.

They got louder, some of them almost demanding to know what he would ask of them.

"Would you hear it, then?" he asked.

The yes was very loud, almost overwhelming.

"It is unprecedented, I know, but we are in strange, strange times," he said, and gestured to me. Without knowing how, I knew he wanted me to stand and come near him. I did, and he put his hand on my shoulder, moving me to stand in front of him. "There is so much strength in this group. So much power, so much determination," he said. Many of them, likely without knowing, seemed to stand up straighter, to square their shoulders. "But there is also caring, comfort, and love. Love that can heal the deepest wounds. That can mend even the most broken of hearts," he said. More than a few of them pulled closer together. "Would you consider taking Aaron, our new friend, who has been so wronged by the straight world...would you consider embracing Aaron into our fold?"

Before I could even become shocked, I was in multiple layers of hugs. The pressure was almost uncomfortable. The heat, though, was powerful. I felt better than I had in quite some time. Through gaps in between necks and shoulders I could just barely see Marcus, arms folded across his chest, smiling. What I didn't see at the time, but in retrospect can picture perfectly was that, just outside the circle, standing nearly 180 degrees opposite from Marcus was Viktor, his arms also crossed, the look on his face not one of pleasure, but deep worry.

VIKTOR

"We're coming in. Lay down on the ground with your hands behind your head and you will not be shot. Fail to follow these instructions and you might be further harmed. I repeat, we're coming in..." the man's voice droned on through the bullhorn. Of course, the bullhorn was overkill. The room wasn't that big. If he had just yelled, I would be able to hear him just fine.

For a second, I almost consider doing as he asks. It would be easy to just surrender. To stop fighting for once. To let them take me into the arms of their giant horrible machine.

To live past this moment.

Then I picture Marcus' face. I remember the way his hand used to rest so lightly on my stomach when we were sleeping against each other. I thought of him dead, the body I had caressed and loved so often lying mangled in a puddle of blood.

"No," I whispered, "not that easy."

Oddly enough, as I'm standing, as I'm squeezing back on the trigger, I'm thinking of that moment when Marcus first brought Aaron in. The gathering. Recruiting had never worked like that before. Normally, we got orders, we picked the kid up, whoever he was, and we moved on. This, though, came straight from Marcus.

I could have stopped it. As the first of my bullets reaches the doorframe, and two of their guns come around that frame pointed at me, I'm thinking I could have stopped all of this.

Not that I want to live forever. That kind of thinking is for the weak. No, I want to make my death count for the cause—that's what I've always wanted, since the second the first soldier ripped my clothes off and made my father watch while they used my body against me, against him. I have dedicated myself to making sure that my revenge is total. I had just always wanted, from the moment I met him, that end to come at Marcus' side. Even this crude gunfight, I'm thinking as their bullets begin to destroy the crate I'd slumped behind, would have been an okay end if Marcus were here beside me.

I don't even feel the first few bullets rip through me.

My right arm is a shredded mess not long after the last pistol I have begins clicking empty. It's still trying to slam bullets at my enemies, still trying to eject spent casings, but nothing is happening.

I could have stopped all of this, I think as one of their bullets rips through my skull, and everything goes black.

MARCUS

File 2618-69370-B
Index: 14-07:29
Room 1159B
Transcript follows:

Harper: Good morning. Jesus. You look like shit.

Prisoner: How kind. Is it morning already?

Harper: (sound of something heavy moving into a chair and a long sigh) How many times do I have to tell you that if you don't start giving us information we need, information we can use, they're going to keep doing this to you.

Prisoner: Something tells me that they will continue doing this for as long as I remain alive whether I tell them anything or not.

Harper: Untrue. We're not monsters. Give us the information we need to prevent further bombings, further harm, and there's even a chance you might live out the rest of your life at one of the resort facilities.

Prisoner: I'm sure that's what your kind told my kind

while we died slowly in the clay pit at Sachsenhausen.

Harper: Unreal. No matter what I tell you, you're always going to come back to your version of events.

Prisoner: My version. I see. I'm sure you didn't come here for a history lesson, Agent Harper, so shall we?

Harper: (sounds of paper shuffling) When we caught you, we recovered a laptop along with the weapons that you and the others had. That laptop had just finished uploading something somewhere. Your crew managed to smash most of it before we could stop you, but there was enough left that we are aware you transferred something from that laptop to somewhere else. I'm guessing we're not exactly talking about a Facebook update. What was it you sent and to where or whom?

Prisoner: I'm sure you've already guessed.

Harper: Did you sent a message or instructions that would activate the next cell's plan?

Prisoner: (quiet laughter)

Harper: Did you give information to the next cell so that they could begin their mission?

Prisoner: Don't you get tired of this? (a long pause) Why is it all our conversations are you asking me to confirm something that you already know or at least suspect?

Harper: (sighing) Just answer the fucking question

Prisoner: Such language.

Harper: What you haven't seemed to put together yet, pal, is that I really am your only friend at this point. I'm the only person looking out for your interests at all. Give me something I can take back to the higher ups and let me try to cut some deals to help you. Something to step in between you and Vikram. Wouldn't you at least like that?

Prisoner: Your little tech weasels have already told you everything they know. I suspect it's quite a lot. You are asking me to confirm what they've said for what? To have that to use against me? In what court? Agent Harper, I keep saying it, and you keep not hearing I don't know what court you think is ever going to hear any of this. There isn't going to be a trial. I've known that since the moment one of your agents either missed my heart or shot close enough to it to take me down without hitting it on purpose. I'm already dead. This facility is my grave. You can't tempt a dead man with anything.

Harper: (sighing again) We're done here.

AARON

The next week or so is a blur. Not only because I'm spending most of it sneaking in and out of my mom's house, only ever there long enough that she sees me and then leaves for work or sees me between the time when she comes in from work and then goes to bed, but also because the rest of the time, when I'm at Marcus' apartment or one of the two apartments next door, where the other boys live, I'm drunk or high or both. They're celebrating me, trying to keep me happy, to help me forget about Daniel. After the first two days, I no longer even try to determine if they've put something in the drinks they hand me. I just know that I don't want this feeling of happiness, this feeling of closeness to end. Some part of me, distant, keeps reminding me that I loved Daniel, and that the touching and kissing and holding that is happening while I'm drunk and stoned with all these other amazing boys and young men is wrong, but as if they can hear it to, the second that voice starts to gain traction, someone hands me a joint or a pipe or a glass of something, and I'm floating again. I never want this feeling to end. I have no idea how my mother never caught me as stumbling out of my mind high and drunk as I would be when she would come home, as incoherent as I would be if she tried to talk to me before leaving. The second I heard her keys lock the front door, though, I was able to get it together enough to shower, put clothes on, and get back to Marcus' apartment. Someone was always either already awake or just now on their way to bed, so they let me in. Eventually, they just wound up giving me a key. I would come in, lock the door behind me, strip off, find a pile of naked bodies, and mold myself into them. They were always warm, and happy to see me. I'd sleep for a few more hours with the rest of them, and then someone was always there to wake me up with a hit of something or a stiff drink and it started all over again.

In the afternoons, Marcus would take me by the elbow and walk me out into the back yard. There, we would spar against one another like we had before. At first I didn't understand it, but about halfway through that first fight after Daniel had been buried, Marcus said, "They took him." I didn't understand what he meant and he swung several more times. I barely got them all blocked. "They took him from you. You weren't strong enough and they took him from you."

I was stunned. How dare he talk about Daniel like that? From somewhere far away, I heard growling. "They took him from you. This whole society is laughing at you and how weak you are," Marcus said. He punched several more times. Looking back I can see that he wasn't really trying to hit me, but at the time, I blocked as if my life depended on it.

"They're laughing at you, and at him," Marcus said, punching again. I blocked and stepped back, but still didn't swing.

"What pansies. What pussies you are. What a weakling little coward he must have been," Marcus said.

I could tell I was growling, but I couldn't stop myself.

"What a little faggot," he said, and I stepped forward and started swinging. I couldn't stop myself. Punch after punch after punch. I found myself grabbing him and trying to throw him to the ground. I hit him in the face. I hit him in the arm. I hit him anywhere I could. I could tell someone was yelling, cursing, crying, but I couldn't tell that it was all me.

I don't know how long that went on, or how none of the neighbors got involved, but when I calmed down, Marcus had me pinned in a bear hug.

"That's it. Use it, don't turn it inward. Use it, don't turn it inward," Marcus kept saying over and over again. "Use it, don't turn it inward," he said again and again. I calmed down slowly, pinned up against him in his arms. After a while my crying slowed, and I could get better breaths. My arms came up slowly and wrapped around him.

"There," he said. "Use it. Don't turn it against yourself."

That became our routine in the afternoons; him pushing me to make sure that, as he put it, "the hate was focused in the right direction—on them instead of yourself." After we would shower together. The first few times, others wanted to come in with us, but Marcus turned them away. We wouldn't have sex, though. Instead, it was just quiet time together, washing one another. These became my favorite times with Marcus.

During those days, too, Marcus was always talking to people. Always speaking to and enlightening us. Always making sure that we were growing more aware by the moment.

"Anytime there is a group of children being cared for in an institutional setting, there is the potential for abuse. Especially if that institution involves straight men. You have to remember—to the average idiot, one of them out there, driving around in their Ford pickup trucks listening to country music and thinking Toby Keith is deep and patriotic, if an adult man has sex with a young boy, they think that's gay. Because they see same sex attraction as vile, anyway. Pedophilia, which psychologists understand as being completely separate from being gay, is the same thing to most people. Fucking idiots walking around out there thinking gay male equals pedophile, even though every statistic you want to use says the men who abuse children most often define themselves as straight. This is what they think of us," he said. "Tell him," Marcus said, looking over at the Ji Yoen.

"In South Korea, if you are talented early, the recording companies will give you a contract," Ji Yoen said. "It's not unusual for a boy or girl to get hired at age 9 or 10. They are then taken away and live communally. Eat together, sleep together, train in music and dance together. Think of an assembly line, only, instead of a car, at the end you have a girl group or a boy band. If a new K-Pop group is unveiled tomorrow, they have actually been in the business for 5 or 6 years, maybe more. And they know that they have a few years of popularity, but the kids that record company has been training that were just a year younger? They're going to be debuting next month. The pressure is enormous.

"The children are always watched. They encourage friendships, and slowly, over the next few years, groups of boys begin to develop. By one year in, there is a minimum amount each child has to know and be able to do. If they do not meet that minimum, they are given special classes. After all, each child represents a sizable investment." He took a sip of his drink, then said, "Of course, during that time, puberty hits, too. So, the cute little kids that the company bought become all elbows and knees and zits. Many of the girls and some of the boys start to be taken for plastic surgery, dental work. Look at the average K-Pop group; they all look like runway models. They are the most beautiful people in a beauty obsessed culture.

"But if one of the kids just isn't getting choreography, and never gets any better at singing, and starts to look so bad that the surgery bills would be enormous, then what is the company to do? They've already paid off the parents. They start thinking about how they're going to get that money back." I could tell he didn't want to say any more, but Marcus put a hand on his shoulder. Ji Yoen set his drink down.

"A few of the producers were already having sex with some of them. Of us," he said, and I tried hard not to say anything. The entire time he'd been talking, it hadn't occurred to me that he might be talking about himself. "Living like that, we stopped thinking of ourselves as kids. We thought of ourselves as grown up, the way kids do when they don't have parents around. The people who were teaching us and making sure we ate lunch didn't seem to think anything was wrong that some of the girls and a few of the boys were favorites of this producer or that one. We all knew what was going on, and no one said anything about it.

"But in the special classes, the remedial classes, it was worse. There weren't many of us in those classes, but almost all of us were yelled at, and hit, and then raped. It wasn't like it was for the other groups—those kids got flowers, or nice watches, or special shoes. In the special class, we got dragged from the bed by our hair.

"Over time, it became obvious which ones were going to be able to catch back up and leave the special classes and which…weren't. On the day they finally made the decision, it was down to three of us—two boys and a girl. The girl and I were loaded on a plane the next day. I thought maybe I was going home; that they'd simply seen that I couldn't dance while singing three-part harmony, and I was going home. I swore to myself I wouldn't tell my family about what had happened to me. Especially not my mother, who was a fuzzy memory at best, at the time.

"They must have put something in the food they gave us on the plane, though, because I slept the entire flight. When we landed, I remember pushing up the window shade and the sunlight was ten times brighter than I'd ever seen it before. Those heat coming up off the tarmac like water," he paused, again. His eyes connected with mine for the first time, and a jolt ran through me. "They'd taken us to Dubai, me and the girl. It's a lot like Las Vegas, in many ways. No one judges anyone else as long as the money is flowing. We were sold, she and I. That was how the company would make its money back. Luckily enough, the person who bought me wasn't actually interested in using me," Ji Yoen said, looking at Marcus and putting his hand on his knee.

"Ji Yoen is the newest of us," Marcus said, "and we're very, very happy he's here." At that, several of the other young men who'd been sitting nearby clapped, and there were shouts of welcome and happiness. I couldn't help but smile at it; they were like a family. I wandered around the party some, always keeping Marcus on the edge of my vision. At one point, I lost him for a time, pretending to be interested as the others said "hello" to me or asked anything. He was all that mattered.

Eventually I found him in the kitchen with another of the young men. "Maybe it's good that he's gone," Marcus said, "did you ever think about that?"

"How can you say that?" the other boy asked.

He looked at me for a moment, and I could tell he was deciding something. Then he said, "He wanted them to accept us because we're just like them. He wanted straight people to see that we're all the same, and so they were being silly. But we're not just like them. Even the normal gays, the ones who aren't like us—they aren't like straight people at all." He stepped closer to the boy, putting his arm around his shoulder, and leaned in closer. "They," he said, gesturing with his chin over his shoulder, "need to accept us because they need to accept us. Or else. That's the message that needs to be sent. That's the only kind they'll ever understand."

"But Doctor Martin Luther King, Jr..." the other boy started.

He closed his eyes and shook his head, "Was it his peaceful protest that won them over? Or was it his death? You and I both know the answer to that. Winston Mendez is more useful to us dead. That was the only message he could ever send that they'd listen to. It was the way he could actually help the movement." He looked up just then and seeing me, winked. "Let's freshen these up, eh?" he asked, then kissed the other boy on the cheek and turned to get them both more vodka.

The night went on. Marcus was always talking. Every once in a while, I would look around to see what other people were doing, and they were always watching him. It's like the whole room was just there to listen to him.

"...I would. I would...when I hear about things like that, so much anger builds up in me that...Do you know what I used to daydream about? Floating above the planet. Like Superman. Only, I'm not floating above the planet feeling peaceful and happy, I'm floating above the planet and I want to unleash destruction. I want the power to become a shining star of obliteration. I want to firebomb the planet in to a cinder. Because the people here are so fucked up...so *fucked up*...there's no fixing it. We have to wipe the slate clean and start over."

I didn't know what to say to that, so I didn't say anything. I could feel him vibrating, though. He was shaking.

"I just think that...that...if they want a god, then I want to give them one. A vengeful god who shows them just what it means to punish the wicked. I want to burn all the straight people away from the planet like the sickness they are," he said, and took a swig of his beer.

I realized I hadn't moved in over an hour. I could have sat there all night just listening, but my body had other ideas. My left leg was all pins and needles. I got up and nearly fell over. As I went past everyone on my way to the bathroom, I felt some of them look at me. The door closed behind me and the fan droned. It felt strange to be in a room by myself so suddenly. After I finished, I went to wash my hands in the sink. The soap was still wet from the last person who'd been in there, but I didn't mind so much. The hand towel was a bit wet already. I looked up and caught sight of myself in the mirror and for a second just stared. I leaned in closer, still looking into my own eyes. A wave of sadness swept over me and I almost started crying. I looked down at the sink and waited until it went away.

Back in the living room, people had shifted around a bit. My seat was already taken by a young black man who had been introduced to me as Abeo. Viktor's eyes were on me. I smiled at him, and sat down on the carpet at the edge of the people. Marcus was still talking, but his eyes found me. "Now, I ask you—what would have happened if one of those guys at Stonewall had really gotten serious? What would have happened if, instead of sitting around and talking about our feelings, and picketing, some of them had decided to get their hands on guns? What would have happened if the GLF would have formed that very night, and not as a protest to the Mattachine assimilationist bullshit, but instead what if—what if they had gone to the local gun store and started taking Christopher Street themselves?" he asked. I could see from the look in his eyes that he wasn't really in the room anymore. They maybe thought about it. Thought about it, maybe. But that's all they did. So here we are, fifty years later, and we're still sitting around in rooms, talking about how we feel, while every day some of us are being kidnapped by our own parents, lobotomized, forced to pray to a God that they tell us hates us. It's bullshit."

I was quiet.

"I don't know about you, but me? I've had enough. Enough of classes about gay authors, enough of testifying about violence committed against us to senators in a congress that votes against us at every fucking turn. Enough of all of it. It's time to do something."

There was a cheer. People raised their cups toward him. The guy next to me elbowed me gently and smiled. Marcus smiled, too, looking around the room slowly, taking each person in. My stomach was tense until his eyes touched mine. It felt like they stayed on me forever.

At some point that seemed much later than anything before, Marcus stood up and then pulled me to my feet by my hands. Then his arm was around my waist. I remember him saying something to the others, and them saying things back to him. Their voices were soft, and I felt really self-conscious and at the same time completely without a care.

Looking back on it, I can see that I was so far beyond drunk that I was barely in my own body.

Moving down a hallway, entering a room, the feeling of Marcus' hands up under my shirt, my shirt coming off. The cold of his shirt against my naked chest. His shirt coming off, his lips at my neck, sounds escaping me that I'd never made before, ever. A part of me pushing so hard against the zipper that I wondered why it hadn't burst, yet. He gave me a small push, and I landed on the bed. The sound of his shirt coming off, then his hands pulling my shoes off, then my socks. His lips and tongue on my toes, my heel. Even though I had sex before, something about this made me feel more naked, vulnerable, than I'd felt those other times.

His hands sliding my pants down without touching the zipper. Then my underwear. His hand on my ankle, pulling one leg free, but leaving them hanging from the other ankle. The entirety of my throbbing in his mouth all in one move. My whole body shuddered, pushing upward, as if trying to put my whole body in his mouth. His hands cupping my pelvis, as if he wanted the same thing, then playing over my thighs. Pushing my knees up onto my chest, then his tongue finding the spot, the center of me, somehow. As he licked and kissed, I felt as though someone had discovered something I'd been trying to hide, something secret and vulnerable inside me. Somewhere in the distance, I heard someone moaning, sighing.

A part of me knew where this was all headed, and that I should make him protect himself, protect me, but I was too far gone. Too scrambled to be good.

He stopped, and I heard someone beg, wordlessly. The sound of his clothes coming off. Then he was back. Then something heavy, and impossible, falling against my thigh. Touching its warmth with my hand, squeezing it. My knees against my chest again. The sound of him spitting. Then his mouth against mine and slowly, slowly, the impossible thing, the thing that could never fit, sliding slowly, slowly, into me, unstoppable. Stretching, terrible pressure that I immediately wanted to stop and at the same time wanted deeper, deeper than even this could possibly go.

It took forever for it to be completely inside. In that moment, we both stopped. One of his hands rested on my own throbbing self, as if my heart rested there, and I knew he could feel every beat of it; one of my toes in his mouth, his other hand holding mine, our fingers wrapped tightly around each other. Then he started to move his pelvis, and something in the world clicked, like a lock opening, then expanded. The definition of every word took on new meanings. We were just starting, and already I knew that my life would never be the same once we were done.

As his hands roamed, as he pushed and pushed himself further and further into me, I began to understand things about my body that I'd never even guessed at before. Things that no one had ever talked about, that I'd never read, but instantly understood.

I wanted us to stay connected like that forever, to never leave this darkness, this bed, to always have him so far in me that his heartbeat became my heartbeat. But I knew from his breathing that soon, this would all be ending. My hands began to trace him desperately, trying to memorize every curve, in case this was the last time. When he breath finally hitched in his throat, and with a groan, he put one arm behind my neck, and shoved his pelvis into me so hard it seemed like he wanted to crawl inside, my whole body contracted, and I left warmth all over my belly and his, even as I felt his own warmth filling me.

He collapsed against me, kissing my neck between giant gulps of air. I felt him slowly relax inside me and the slippery opening of myself. When he rolled over to lie next to me, I could still feel him inside me, though he wasn't anymore. His left arm slid over my chest, and his left hand grasped my right arm loosely. He made a noise that I knew asked if I was okay. I made a noise meaning that I was. He kissed my earlobe, and we lay like that until I fell asleep.

That was the first night that I didn't go home. When I woke the next day, disturbingly sober, Marcus wasn't there. Alone in that bed and sober in the light of the morning, I knew I had to get in touch with mom. She'd be worried. I got up, got dressed and borrowed someone's sunglasses from the dining room table. I stumbled home, leaning against the front door to wait for my eyes to adjust.

On the kitchen table there was a note:

Aaron,

I knew that this time was going to come. Despite what you might think, I remember what it was like to be a teenager. So, I'll tell you like my dad told me—I worry. Don't take my worry as some sign that I don't trust you, but I'm a parent, and that's what we do. So, while it is okay with me that you're starting to stretch out, to have new experiences, that doesn't mean that you can just disconnect entirely. You will call, sober or not, to let me know if you are going to be home from now on. If you don't call by the time I normally go to bed, I will start calling morgues, hospitals, the police, etc. That can lead to legal trouble for you, do you understand? You don't want that. I don't want that. So, from now on, you will call.

I love you,
Mom.

It hurt me to know she'd worried. I felt like shit.

I was never supposed to call her at work, but I felt like I had to this time. It'd been so long, though, I didn't know the number anymore. I had to look it up off the magnet on the refrigerator.

"Coleman, Whitkerson, and Powell," the woman who picked up said.

"Sheila Miller, please," I said.

"May I tell her who's calling?"

"Aaron,"

"One moment," the woman said and the line clicked over to the wordless soft jazz channel.

"Aaron," Mom said as the line clicked over again.

"Hi," I said. It was only then that I noticed I hadn't even bothered to take the sunglasses off. I was standing in a completely dark house, in an even darker kitchen (no windows in there) with sunglasses on.

"Where were you?"

"Marcus' house," I said before I thought about it. She'd never heard me talk about Marcus before and had certainly never met him.

"Who's that?" she asked.

"A new friend. He lives here in the complex," from experience, I knew that the closer I could keep it to the truth, the less trouble there would be. My mom wasn't exactly a human lie detector, but she was fairly good.

"I haven't met him," she said.

"No," I said.

"Look, I meant what I said in the note. If this is the new status quo, those are the rules. Got it?" she said.

I could hear how hard this was for her in her voice. I tried for a second to think about what it must mean to start to let go of someone that you care about, but I could see that road lead directly to the feelings about Daniel, and so I cut it off. I imagined a giant concrete wall slammed between me the rest of that road.

"Yes," I said.

"Okay. I love you," she said. I knew she wanted to grill me, to get details, to demand information but was stopping herself.

"I love you, too," I said, and I hung up. I stood there in that empty kitchen, feeling the weight of the empty house around me. We'd never even gotten a cat. I don't know why that thought occurred to me in that moment, but it did, and it made me cry. My back slid down the wall and the sunglasses fell off. I huddled there next to the refrigerator sobbing, crying so hard no sound was coming out.

After a time, I wiped my face the best I could with the heel of my hand and waited for the final hiccupping sobs to taper off. Eventually I put the glasses back on and stood. I went upstairs and showered, hovering on the edge of crying again the entire time. I tried not to look at all the places on my body that were now a bit bruised or marked. I tried not to think about how much more comfortable my body felt than it ever had before because of how many people had touched it, caressed it, kissed it. Standing there, nearly scalding hot water running down my shoulders and over my stomach and down my thighs, it was unavoidable—I was a completely different person than the one that had stepped into this shower at the beginning of summer.

I might as well not even have the same name, I thought as I toweled off.

I dug through my closet to find the duffle bag that I'd gotten three Christmases ago. It was brand new, even though it was that old, because I'd never used it. I stuffed a few changes of clothes into it and my music player. My hand hovered on my laptop for a moment, but I knew if I took it, if I opened it, I'd go straight to Daniel's YouTube page, and I would break, so I left it. Next to it was the CD I'd written "U2" on.

Everything in the room reminded me of how things had been just a few weeks ago, of Daniel. I remembered him saying how he liked that they used their power and money to help others. Asking if any other big music stars had the balls to try to help others.

"With or without you," I felt like whispering for some reason, so I did, then repeated it, almost singing the notes but my throat closed up. I turned and walked out of my room and down the stairs.

I locked the front door behind me, feeling like it might be the last time. That the person who used to live here didn't even exist anymore. I didn't know if I'd be back or not, but I had a feeling I wouldn't.

I put my sunglasses on, turned, and walked away from that door.

VIKTOR

Toward the end, I got impatient. I could tell it would not be long before Marcus told the boy what was going to happen. Asked him to join us.

One morning, when he was sneaking back into the apartment, I was waiting on the stairs. As he turned around from closing the door, I stopped him before he could get his shoes off.

"With me," I said, my hand against his elbow.

He blinked but did not resist. I walked him back out the front door and all the way to one of the jeeps we'd been using.

"In," I said. He hesitated a moment, but then he must have seen the look on my face. He got in. I started, backed out, and drove us out of the complex, along the side road to one of the parking lots nearby. When I stopped the jeep and turned it off, I got out. He waited a moment, then did the same.

"You are becoming one of us very quickly," I said coming around the front. "If that's going to happen, then there are things you need to know. That I need to know that you know before it goes too far to turn back."

"I thought I already was one...one of you," he said.

"It's mostly done, but not completely. Not yet."

"I don't understand."

I looked away from the boy. For a moment, I wonder if I am monster enough to tell the truth to a face this sweet. I decide that I am. "Marcus had planned to kill your boyfriend. He and I killed Winston Mendez." I closed my eyes. Then I open them.

The world went quiet.

He dry heaved twice, then turned away quickly and vomited.

I walked back toward the doors. I pulled a bottle of water from compartment between the seats and took it back to him.

"I don't believe you," he said after a moment.

"That's not true," I replied, "you believed me the instant I said it. In fact, some part of you already knew. Some part of you already knows everything I'm about to tell you, but there's also a part of yourself that is thinking, 'Things like this don't happen in real life.' That filter everyone has that tells them conspiracy doesn't exist, and that sixth sense is an illusion." I reached out and took the boy's hand as he stood up. We both leaned back against the hood.

"Why would he do that, though?" Aaron asked. Some part of my brain was amazed at the lack of anger he was showing. I had expected him to lash out. There was no anger, no incredulousness, nothing.

"Initially, Marcus wanted your boyfriend," I said.

"Wanted...for...what?" he asked.

"Not what you're thinking. Something else. That will all be shown to you soon. But the other boy—,"

"Daniel," he said, angry that someone could refer to someone he'd cared for so much, who had been so specific, in such a generic way.

"...Daniel," I said, "had the video channel. Originally, that was the plan. The plan has changed, though."

"What plan? What plan, and why did it change?" he asked.

"You," Viktor said. He shook his head, "The funny part is, you don't even know it, do you? How you affect people?" I shook my head again, and looked down. "Do you think Marcus fucks just anyone?"

The boy had been taking a swallow of water, but paused, shocked. He was, no doubt, wondering how I knew?

"Yes, I know. Have known since before it happened. Since we're all connected, he talked to all of us before he decided to bring you in."

"Bring me in?"

"To the group. Before he gave you the gift that would make you one of us, he asked us all if we were okay with it. Because it meant that, should something happen to him, we'd still accept you. Look out for you."

"This...this is all sounding a little...just a little too much like a stupid vampire TV show."

I laughed, and he nearly dropped the bottle. In all our time doing this, I had never thought of it that way. "It does, doesn't it?" I asked, still smiling. "And, in a way, it is like that. Connected by blood. The same things swimming around in my blood now swimming around in yours."

"What are you talking about?"

I didn't say anything for a moment, then looked directly at the boy. His eyes met mine. A shiver ran thought him. "You've had sex with people other than Marcus, right?"

"Yes," he said. I had a feeling he meant with the other boy, Daniel, but didn't press. I could tell by the edge in his voice he thought of this as a confrontation.

"Did you use protection with them?" I asked, and in his eyes I saw it, a flash of insight—he could see, in some small way, where this was going. He nodded. "And yet, did you use any with Marcus?" I asked in a tone that meant I knew he hadn't. "Why do you suppose you did that? Should we call it teenage lust making you stupid? We could. But we could also say that on some level, you knew what would happen."

"What would happen?" he asked.

"He gave it to you."

I watched his eyes move, the tilt of his chin change. I saw him working through what I'd just said. "Marcus has HIV," he said after a few moments.

I looked away, then turned back to him. "We all do." He let that hang there for a moment. A wind came through catching his hair and my collar.

"It's what binds us all together. The way we're all connected," I said.

"That's—I don't understand; that's not...right..."

"But isn't it? Most of us already had it before we joined up. When someone is holding you down, they generally don't take the time to put a condom on. But it was one of the first guys who figured that if we all wanted to connect...if we really wanted to be connected with each other, then that was the way. Each of us has the same disease running through us."

"But—different strains—"

"That's why we all have sex with each other. The warrior orgy. Lots of ancient cultures did it. It builds powerful bonds between warriors when they're also lovers."

"So, now—now I have it?" he asked.

"Yes," I said, "You have Marcus' strain inside you for sure. Maybe some of the rest of ours, too."

"Now I'm one of you? I'm one of you," he whispered. "Is this why you are here? To tell me this" he asked.

"Because things are coming together very quickly, now, and I see where it's all heading. Where it's been headed for a long time." He looked at his feet. "I don't know what to do." I inhaled, then exhaled, then said, "Johnny Gosch, Paul Bonacci, Steven Staynor, even, in a way. It's—I dunno—do you know what brainwashing is?" I asked.

"What?"

"Brainwashing. I don't mean the way they show it on stupid TV shows, but the real stuff. Do you know anything about it?"

He shrugged.

"There are people who want soldiers, terrorists, assassins, slaves... whatever the fuck you want to call it. They want a person that they can control. Totally control. Make them do whatever they want. Government eggheads have been toying around with this shit for a long, long time. At least going back to Mengele in World War II, probably longer." I kicked at a small rock near the toe of my shoe.

"Eventually they hit on this idea they called Monarch. They always came up with cutsie names for their shit. Monarch programming takes a person, usually very young, way younger than you," I said, looking out to the horizon, then back at my shoe, "and...and hurts them. Hurts them bad. That's what it was in the beginning, but you see after a while they discovered that they didn't have to do that part of the work. All they had to do was look the other way while people who were already hurting kids did their thing. Then they could just swoop in and scoop up the kid after. The best part is that, these huge networks of sick fucks could operate practically out in the open because no one wanted to believe that these things could be so organized. They want to believe that a guy who wants to fuck kids is a lone monster. No one wants to think that there might be a whole collection of these kinds of guys, or that they are organized." I looked at the boy full on, waiting for him to say something. I could tell he wanted to argue with me, but just before the word "no" came out, I could see he realized that reaction was exactly what I was talking about.

"Ultra violent men doing horrible things to kids being protected by the spooks. Auctions of kids to diplomats and businessmen who only came in the county to buy three more little boys to replace the three that they'd already nearly destroyed last month. Unchartered private flights filled with every kid that went missing in the whole country during the month of January. Think of the most horrible things you could think of to do to a kid, sexually or otherwise, and you might come close to the kinds of things these men did at parties. Pictures, even. Then, when the kids are done, alive but so horribly screwed up that some wind up with multiple personalities or whatever the shrinks are calling it now, all the spooks have to do is scoop them up." He shifted a bit on the bumper, then said, "Trauma leads to dissociation, dissociation leads to the person being more easily, more deeply implanted hypnotically, and" he snapped, "just like that, you have yourself someone who'll pull any trigger, cut any throat, fuck anyone to get their secrets while they chat afterwords."

"Wait," he said after a moment, "were you—?" he started to ask.

"No," I said. "Marcus."

He froze.

"When Marcus did the job they wanted him to do, they dumped him on the street. He drifted for a while, but these...other guys who reach out to street kids, get them organized, they found him. Helped him. Then he helped them to find others."

"You," he said.

"Me," I said. "Thing is, it didn't take long for him to be a leader. He already has all this training, he can do these incredible things," I said, my voice going quieter without my control. "Once we found out about Marcus, and what they did, we started looking for these kids, ourselves. Find them before the spooks can or get them away early enough to help them."

"But," he started, "How could...? How can all this be happening? I mean—here?"

"It didn't start in America. It couldn't. We've never really seen the level of systematic violence that it takes to create something like this. It started in Arab countries. Syria, Pakistan. Places where soldiers line up to rape little boys in front of their fathers and laugh about it. Because they know that honor demands the father then kill the boy, or else he be...dirtied...himself. So they're raping two people at once. It takes living in a place where a kid who should be in seventh grade gets snatched off the street by grown men and tortured until he's begging for his mother, and then dropped off at his family's doorstep, unable to walk ever again. It took people from places like this to create this thing. But it didn't take long for those they met to figure out it could work in other places. And then those people met others. And they met others. So, here we are. Now, Marcus has met you.

"Do you remember, at the party, when Ji Yoen talked about being bought and saved? He didn't say it, because we all already knew, but he wasn't talking about Marcus. Marcus is in control here, but this whole thing goes a lot deeper than just us, just him. It's organized into cells, each doing its task, to complete an overall objective."

I could see it finally click into place for him. It had been staring him in the face the entire time, but he hadn't seen it.

"It's..." he started.

"It's what?" I asked.

"It's a...a...terrorist group?"

"What's the difference between a terrorist and a freedom fighter?" I asked him. He looks away again, his eyes going glassy. "Seems to me," I went on, "that the only difference is which end of the rape someone is on. All these redneck fucks who think they've got the world fucking figured out, who love to throw around the word terrorist like they love to throw around the word nigger, it seems to me all of these Fox-News loving motherfuckers who pine away for the glory days of President Bush like he was an ex who wouldn't give them more than a handjob in high school—it seems to me they'd feel a whole lot different about the kinds of things that get labeled 'terrorism' if someone rolled a row of tanks down Veterans Boulevard." He makes eye contact again, and I say, "The important question is this: will you help us, now that you know? Or will you turn us in?"

"If...if I told, what would happen?" he asked.

I looked at the ground between us. "Someone would have to stop you."

"You?" Aaron asked.

"Maybe," I said.

"Oh," he said. "I…I need time to think," he said, "and I want to talk to Marcus."

"Most people do. Thing is, this whole thing is coming together really quickly. He sent me to do this. To talk to you," I said. "He wants an answer now, because we're out of time."

He was shaking, and I could see his mind racing. I've seen this before: He's thinking "If I could only talk to Marcus, I'd be able to make sense out of all of this. If I could just hear his voice, he could make me understand." For it to work, though, for it to *really* work, he had to make the decision himself. Anything else would mean disaster at the end.

"You're saying to yourself that there's still a chance," I said after I'd been silent for a while. "You think that if you walk away, things can go back to being normal. You can go back to watching stupid reality TV or whatever it is you do, and all of this will just go away. Let me explain something to you that I don't think you understand—none of any of this makes any sense. And I don't mean that in some 'I've-read-too-many-books-by-Camus' kind of way.

"I mean that right now, as you sit here, there are people who commit suicide because they can't find anyone to love them, and in that same world, the one you live in, there are also people who are desperate to love someone but can't. You live in a world where there are teenage boys auctioning themselves off on websites, who are begging to be bought, sold, tortured…*killed*. Imagine for a second a forty-year-old man living in an apartment typing a suicide note because he wants a young man to love and care for and yet none will ever look twice at him because he is old, fat, slow. He's typing that note on a computer and right on the other side of that paper thin apartment wall is a teenage boy who wants desperately to be cared for by an older man but can't ever even look at one because older men are told if they even look at someone in their teens, they are some kind of monster. So, because he's kept from finding loving, healthy relationships of the kinds he wants, he turns to the internet and winds up advertising himself for a master/slave relationship. That older man winds up killing himself, and the boy winds up killed because the master he found invited ten of his buddies over for a party and they overdosed the kid while using him for hours and hours on end."

"Why are you telling me all this?" he asked, trying hard to keep the tears in.

"This is what we do—we find these people, and we deprogram them, then we show them a way to make a difference. We work against the idiocy that this culture has constructed for itself. We make strong soldiers out of the lives that this idiotic culture has left for dead. Somehow, though, we get called the bad guys."

"But—," he started to say but stopped.

"And so, here you are."

"For what?" he asked

I looked at me for a long time, then said, "Because we need you."

His shaking got worse, then slowly stopped. "Yes," he whispered.

I looked up and into his eyes.

"Yes." he nodded.

"Come on," I said, walking around to the driver's side door. "There's a lot to do, and we have to get started."

AARON

I walked in to Marcus' apartment, letting myself in with my key.

I slipped off my shoes as was customary and set the duffle bag down near the stairs where people's backpacks and messenger bags tended to accumulate.

"Hello?" I called out.

"Back here," Marcus said. He was back in one of the bedrooms. I found him alone in front of the beat up old laptop that he used.

"You see this?" Marcus says, pointing at the screen.

I read a few lines of a profile and it hits me. This isn't a dating site. The boy here, pictured in a normal sweater and khakis, standing in a museum lobby, is asking for someone to rape him. He wants someone to take his virginity by rape, and then to strangle him to death. I read another profile, and this boy says he's shy, and then asks for someone to take him to their house and make him a slave. He says he wants no freedom. The whole page is like that. I can see at the bottom of the page that there are at least 20 more pages. I look at Marcus.

"This is what their system turns us in to. This is what they make of us. They tell us we're sick, that we're perverts. Then they put us through the system that they have, which turns us into damaged goods. Then, when they see how damaged we are, they call us perverts. This is what they do to us," he says. I lean back in the chair.

"I was just like this," he says, quietly, standing up. "Confused. Angry. Hurting. I thought I wanted someone to end it. The first man who came along did try to kill me, but another one stepped in. He told me how my desire for extreme harm was their fault. He showed me how to get above it. To put the anger where it belongs, instead of letting them make me destroy myself. Instead, he showed me how to destroy them."

"So, each month, I try to save a few of them, just like he saved me. Not many can get beyond their programming. They end up tied up in a closet in some fat old fuck's house out on some deserted road in southern Illinois or wherever. But a few...a few see the light, and they get free."

"How many..." I started, but my voice failed. "How many... groups?...like yours are there?"

"I lost count after a hundred. There's a book with the contact numbers, addresses, that sort of thing. Viktor keeps telling me we have to adopt more of a cell model. Something he read in a book about each group having limited contact with other groups. It makes sense, but I keep telling him part of what we do is brotherhood. Loving each other when the world tries to kill us. He thinks I'm a moron, but I think it makes sense."

I looked at him. He looked back at me, and I felt like we were seeing each other for the first time ever. "What about you, Aaron. Are you going to let them destroy you, or are you going to put the anger where it belongs?" He turned to me and put his hands on my hips, pulling me onto his lap.

"Will you help us, Aaron? Will you help us get revenge for what they did to all of us, to millions of us around the world right now, as we speak?" I looked away but he put his hand on my chin, gently turning my face toward his. "Will you help us get revenge for Daniel?"

"Yes," I said. I'd have done anything for him at that point.

He smiled and then kissed me, pressing me close to him. Then he picked me up and took me to the other bedroom.

"Just imagine it," Marcus whispered, his thumb tracing the top of my shoulder. "Imagine a world where we were equal. Where none of this was necessary. I think about it all the time."

I made a noise in agreement and snuggled into his chest.

"I picture it, sometimes. Especially America. I picture it," he said and sighed. The warmth we generated lying together was almost uncomfortable in spots, but because it was ours, it made me feel loose and free. "Imagine an America where the Supreme Court ruled that all marriages were equal. That's one that makes me happy to think about. I think about the President coming out to that little podium, the one they always use for him to make a comment on breaking news...where is that one? The Rose Garden?" He stopped for a moment.

"I don't know," I whispered without opening my eyes.

"Imagine the President of the United States standing at that little podium saying something like 'Today, justice has arrived like a thunderbolt.' Maybe he'd even be black, like that senator that ran against the old man the first time. Imagine that—a black president announcing that same sex marriages were equal to hetero marriages in the eyes of the law. What an amazing world that would be." His tone was far away, as if whispered from another room. It was comforting and disturbing all at the same time. He was quiet for a long time, and I thought he had fallen asleep, but then he whispered, "a world where no one was killed, no one was raped, no one was kicked out into the street, where no one was beaten for who they love. That's what all this is about. That's why we fight."

I drifted off, then. In my dream that night, I was closed in a straightjacket in a giant, empty warehouse.

I heard a lock click, and then he stepped back. "Done," he said. I tried to move my arms, but they were pinned by the material snugged around them. He walked from behind me to the little box hanging from the cord. His eyes locked on mine. "To really be one of us, you have to face some of your worst fears. We all did." He turned the box toward me and I could see one button labeled "up" and the other labeled "down." "There's a cable connected to the back of the jacket that I just locked you in. That cable is connected to a winch up there," he said, looking up. I followed his gaze to see that there was a motor up in the rafters. "In a second, I'm going to press the button and you're going to be hauled upward. I know you're afraid of heights, so this is going to be hard for you." My ears began to pound from the blood rushing to them. My breathing increased. "Worse, after you're about this high," he said, holding his other hand near his waist, "I'm going to flip you upside down. You're going to hang, upside down, high enough up to activate your fear." I couldn't control my breath. I wanted out—of the jacket, the garage, everything. His eyes were locked on mine, though, and I couldn't speak. "And this isn't the only time this is going to happen. We're going to do this and keep doing it until you aren't afraid anymore. Then, I'm going to throw you off a building." He walked over to me, and it was only then that I could hear myself wimpering. I tried to stop, but that only made it worse. He pulled me close and kissed my forehead. "Shhhh. I'm here. You're going to get through this." I pushed my head forward to try to nuzzle against him, but I heard a "click" and the sound of a motor.

I was being hauled upward.

I woke to find him asleep next to me. His powerful chest. His fuzzy stomach. His powerful and slim hips. I listened to him breathe for a time, then slipped back off to sleep.

Days later, I don't know how many. I was drunk and high less often, but everything was still a haze. I had been home less and less. During those days, Marcus and Viktor and the others had told me a great deal about what they did.

One morning I woke expecting to see Viktor and Richard, whom I'd gone to bed with next to me, but instead I found Marcus and I alone in the room. He was naked and hard and before I could get my brain straightened out, my legs were over his shoulders and he was inside me. My eyes rolled back in my head and for a time, there was only my body.

As he finished and then rolled away from me, I rolled with him so that I was against his chest again.

"Oh?" he said.

"I don't want you away from me," I whispered, pulling his other arm over my shoulder.

He said something under his breath that I could tell was Russian, but I didn't understand it. "What?" I asked.

"Nothing," he said in the same tone I'd heard when he was sure he'd won an argument.

"Do you like it?" I asked.

"Like what?" he asked in return.

"You know—what you do. Hurting people."

"What I do, what *you* do, now, too—it is more than just hurting people. That is only a part of it."

I was playing with his fingers. "It's fun at times, I guess, knowing that I'm getting revenge for things these people have done, but what you do is more."

He sighed, and for a moment I closed my eyes, feeling him breathe against me. "Things are bad for you, here, yes; but remember that where I come from, where the others come from—things are very bad. Being willing to hurt someone before they hurt you might mean the difference between living and dying. This is something I do not like, and I take no joy in it, but it is the truth."

"So why are you here?" I asked.

"Because enough is enough," he said, "and there has to be a Malcom X," he whispered.

"What?" I asked, and turned over to face him.

He looked at me for a second like he was making a decision, then looked at the ceiling. For a moment, I feared he wasn't going to tell me. That we'd come all this way, and he'd finally decided that I couldn't be told something.

"Martin Luther King. He taught peaceful resistance. Like Ghandi. But the thing is, for whomever is teaching peace to make an impact, there has to be the other thing. The dominant culture has to see that if they don't take the carrot, then someone is going to use the stick," he had that tone in his voice again, and I could tell he was quoting someone. "For Martin Luther King's message of peace to work, the whites at the time had to see Malcom X. The Black Panthers. The whites had to know that they were being offered a choice—peace, or war." He took my hand, squeezing it lightly. "There has to be a carrot, a stick, and a martyr. That's the only way to make a difference." He let go of my hand.

Instantly, the fog that I'd been living in for months cleared, and I saw it. My head moved back on my neck, and my eyes widened. "You—you and Viktor—the rest—"

He nodded.

I didn't move, afraid that the slightest shift from me would stop him from saying what I knew he would say next. What I prayed he wouldn't say. What I needed him to say.

"We couldn't wait around for some other group to pick up the slack, though. We knew we needed to control all three elements," he said, "we manufacture the threats ourselves. We also control the ones speaking peace."

"And you killed—" I started but couldn't finish.

"*We* killed Winston Mendez," he said, kissing my neck and putting his forehead against my ear. "The biggest threat, you see, are the do nothing assimilationists. They see our struggle, and they secretly wish us well, but they do nothing. They don't speak out, they don't pick up a gun, they don't help us. And if they aren't helping us, they're even more in the way than the straights. No. No lukewarm support. No more Twitter activists," he said, his arm pulling me in tighter.

"Do you love me?" I asked.

"You're one of us, now. I love you as much as I love myself."

We fell asleep tangled in each other.

MARCUS

File 2618-69370-B
Index: 15-09:29
Room 1159B
Transcript follows:

(sound of door opening)
(quiet for several minutes)
(sound of door opening again)

Harper: Vikram.

Vikram: Harper.

Harper: Look, you guys you've got to stop doing this.

Vikram: Doing what?
Harper: He's drugged all to hell and back again. I am not going to be able to get anything out of him until tomorrow. I thought we were supposed to be working together on this thing.

Vikram: We are.

Harper: Sure we are. Look, level with me. How much longer until you guys you know

Vikram: Until we what?

Harper: "Extraordinary rendition."

Vikram: I'm not sure I know what you mean, Agent Harper.

Harper: Come on; I just need to know what kind of timeline I'm up against. I'm getting information, but it's going slowly.

Vikram: For you, maybe.

Harper: Oh? What do you guys have?

Vikram: Those documents are being looked at now; they'll be along to you shortly.
Harper: Shortly? I'm trying to prevent another incident. I need to know what's going on now.

Vikram: Are you saying you don't feel like we're trying to prevent more incidents, as well?
(quiet for a few minutes)

Harper: I know you guys have drugs that would leave him more conscious than this. Could I at least ask that you use some of those next time?

Vikram: I'm not sure there's going to be a next time

for this particular detainee.

Harper: Aha! See, I knew it. You guys are going to be taking him soon.
(more quiet)

Harper: If you're not here to help or give me any information, then what are you here for? Why'd you come in the room?

Vikram: I can't say.

Harper: Can't? Or won't?

Vikram: Does it matter?
Harper: What are you doing? Checking his pulse? Why?

Vikram: (after a moment) It's not important. Good day, Agent Harper.
(sound of door opening and closing)
(quiet for a few moments)

Harper: God damn it.
(sound of door opening and closing)

15-11:31

Harper: Good morning.

Prisoner: Good morning.

Harper: Look, I won't bullshit you there's been word from the judge, and it isn't good.

Prisoner: I never expected anything else.

Harper: (paper shuffling) "it is the judgment of this court (someone laughs) of this court that Prisoner #9370-B, known as Marcus Rudenko, has committed sufficient criminal action to warrant the maximum penalty of death " It goes on, but I imagine you get the idea.

Prisoner: Again, I never expected anything else. It's hard to be upset by something that I have always considered inevitable.

Harper: Yeah.
(a long silence)

Harper: They're going to decide when very soon, but I wouldn't expect that it would be too much longer.

Prisoner: No, I wouldn't think they'd want me around too much longer. What is going to happen to Viktor and the others?

Harper: (a moment of quiet) There never were any others.

Prisoner: Viktor?

Harper: They never got him back to stable. He died a few hours after he was taken into custody.

Prisoner: (a long quiet) I see. You lie very well. Is that a skill you're proud of?
Harper: I did what I had to do.

Prisoner: Keep telling yourself that and maybe someday you'll actually believe it.

Harper: People's lives were on the line. I did what I had to do.

Prisoner: You lie very well to everyone but yourself, I should have said. You don't believe that for a second.

Harper: It worked, though.

Prisoner: Yes, telling me that someone I cared for more than you could ever imagine one human being could care for another was alive and that my cooperation would entice you to help him in order to get what you wanted, that worked. It doesn't matter, though.

Harper: I would have thought you'd be more angry.

Prisoner: I am angry, but I don't need to try something futile like coming across this table and breaking your windpipe and then pressing my entire weight down on your chest so that I can look into your panicked eyes as you die slowly. No, I can remain calm because whatever you've done to me, whatever your idiot fat, limp-dicked, balding old white men leaders have done to others like me, it won't matter. You can't stop it now.
Harper: Stop what? What are you smirking for? We've got your whole group. It's all over.

Prisoner: No reason.

Harper: No, you might as well tell me.

Prisoner: Okay. Why not? I'm smiling because I'm happy.

Harper: And why are you happy?

Prisoner: Because 24 hours after Viktor failed to show up at the specified time and place to give his report? Another group activated.

Harper: What?

Prisoner: In your stupid straight media, you call them "cells." What, did you think we were acting alone? (there is the sound of a laugh) You weren't paying attention. There are more of us than you can imagine. And by taking us in the way you have, all you have done is activate the next group. Maybe even the next two I seem to remember there was some talk of that before

Harper: Who are they? What are their objectives?
Prisoner: Do you think for a second anyone was stupid enough to tell me?

Harper: Tell me who they are! Tell me what their objectives are!

Prisoner: (sound of laughter)

Harper: Tell me!
(sound of something solid hitting something metal once, then again, then again, sound of the door opening and a scuffle)

End of Transcript

VIKTOR

Two hours after we hear the bomb go off, it's time.

"A moment of silence," Marcus says. We all bow our heads as we've done time and time again.

"Alright," Marcus says softly, "Our work here is done. I want pack out and vehicle loading done in twenty-five minutes. We will be outside city limits before they have the fire under control. Move," he says. It makes my heart lift to hear the voice of Marcus, *my* Marcus, again. All the boys break and begin moving between this apartment and the other one. They are loading the two ancient black SUVs quickly and quietly.

"Who?" I ask Marcus as he rolls his swords slowly and deliberately in their cloth.

He pauses without looking at me. "You. Ji Yoen. Richard. You'll take the satellite phone and the laptop."

I'm rocked back by this. I knew it would be Richard. I thought that it would be Ji Yoen. But me?

"Once we've separated, you'll make contact to start the next group, as well. There's been a decision to use the momentum."

"But—," I started.

He stopped what he was doing and stepped toward me. He put his hand on my shoulder and our eyes locked. "You're ready. It's time."

"But—," I started again.

"Loaded," Richard said from the patio.

Marcus shook my shoulder, then let go and turned back to his swords.

"Richard," I said without looking at him, "Get Ji Yoen, the sat phone, and the laptop. We're truck 1. Everyone else in truck 2."

"On it," he said without asking anything, as if he'd already done the math himself. Outside, I heard both of the old Suburbans come to life.

"It's...it's been..." I started. Marcus looked up as he tucked the last fold in and I could tell he'd already closed himself off. We were already done.

I nodded, lowering the mask I'd worn a million times before, and turned on my heel. I'd seen this same ritual played out more than once, and I knew how it had to go. Mission over everything else. The mission was all. I tried to ignore that the other boys were watching me as I swung into the battered old truck's passenger seat. As soon as the door was closed, I said "Let's go." Richard pulled the black dinosaur into gear and we backed away. Ji Yoen already had the laptop open and the sat phone sitting on the other chair nearby. I tried to not look in the rearview and failed. Ji Yoen slid forward and handed me my sunglasses. I put them on.

As we rounded the bend, though, moving toward the exit/entrance of the complex, three much newer large black SUVs came screeching in. They had flashing red and blue lights blazing. Richard looked over at me and I looked back at Ji Yoen. He slid on his knees to the third row of seats and turned back to me, two large .45s in his hand. I took both, keeping one and handing the other to Richard, who was turning us out onto the main road. I knew better than to look for anything bigger than the pistol—as per the rules of a split, most of the weapons went with the larger group, leaving the smaller, newer branch to find its own equipment. These pistols and my old swords were all we had.

As soon as we could no longer see the Federal SUVs, for that was surely what they were, Richard punched the accelerator.

"Make the call," I said, moving back to the third row myself.

Ji Yoen picked up the sat phone and dialed. Richard was weaving the battered relic we were in through traffic as best he could, knowing that we didn't have long before they found we weren't at the safe houses and then started to come after us. My mind wanted to waste time wondering how they had found out, wondering why they had chosen today of all days and not tomorrow when we would all have been safely away. My mind wanted to waste time wondering if they already had Marcus or if he and the others had made it away out the other entrance/exit to the complex.

Instead, I checked the clip, sliding it back home while looking out the back windows.

"Anything?" Richard yelled over the sound of the old V8 being pushed to its limits.

"Not yet," I yelled back.

Ji Yoen put the phone down and looked to me. I looked back. He nodded.

"Start the upload," I said. He nodded again, and tried to balance the generic laptop on his knees as Richard wove the bulky truck through traffic.

At least that had been taken care of.

The mission was all.

"I can't get connection," Ji Yoen said.

"Shit," I said both to that as well as the fact that I could now clearly see, though still quite a way back in traffic, a Federal SUV, lights blaring, clearly chasing us.

"One," I yelled to Richard.

"I see," he yelled back.

"Keep trying," I said in Korean to Ji Yoen. He nodded without looking up from the screen.

The Federal SUV was gaining on us. Though nearly as big as the rusted out hulk we were in, it was newer, and still had its specially made interceptor engine in it. It swung around a bank of cars into the empty oncoming lane for a moment and as it did so, I saw that there was another identical truck just behind it.

"Two," I yelled to Richard.

"Shit," he said.

One we might have gotten away from through speed or evasion. Two lowered those chances exponentially. All three of us knew it.

I slid on my knees up to the front, bracing myself against the driver's seat sideways so I could see our pursuers and Richard. "We're going to have to ditch and split up."

I watched as the realization came over him, too. He swung his eyes to mine for a second then back to the road. He nodded. At that moment I saw the sign that said we were just a quarter of a mile from the on-ramp to the interstate where our chances of making it would have been better.

"Hang on!" he yelled and slammed the wheel to the right. The weight of the truck slid toward him, and for a split second we were nearly on two wheels. I wasn't even paying attention to the number of small crashes we'd caused. I knew better than to hope that the agents hadn't seen our sudden right turn or that we would lose them. As per our training, our only chance at this point was to ditch the truck in such a way as to cause chaos and split, lowering their chances of getting us all.

"I've got signal. Upload starting," Ji Yoen said. We looked at each other. I shook my head "no." There wasn't going to be enough time. But maybe some of the data might make it through. Maybe enough. The call had gone through. That was what mattered. I picked up the sat phone and opened the back, sliding the card out. It was an ancient model, like the trucks, like everything we had.

The agents were now right up on us. If the windshields hadn't been tinted, I'd be able to see the front seats of both. It wouldn't be long before they tried some kind of maneuver. I figured we had maybe twenty minutes, probably less. No doubt there was a helicopter already inbound.

"Ears," I said. Ji Yoen covered his ears with his hands while Richard did his best to hunker his shoulders up to cover his. I put the card on top of the body of the phone, set them both on the floor of the truck, and shot them. Then I rolled down the window and tossed both out.

"Fifteen percent," Ji Yoen said.

"Coming up on it," Richard said. He'd found a spot, then, that he thought likely.

I moved back to the front. Richard had picked a truck stop that backed up to a deserted desert lot on one side, and a series of smaller buildings with a large junk yard behind them on the other. Not a perfect choice, but as good as we were going to get.

"Keep it going as long as you can," I said to Ji Yoen. He nodded, checking his own clip.

"No airbags," Richard said.

"Okay," I said. I looked to make sure that Ji Yoen had heard. He began buckling his seat belt.

I leaned over and began buckling Richard in while he drove.

"I'm sorry," he said.

"None of this is your fault," I said, sliding the buckle closed.

I slid into the second-row seat beside Ji Yoen and buckled myself in. I reached for one of the handles near the roof. "Okay," I said.

Richard gunned the engine far past the red line and veered for the truck stop. He smashed side-on through the front of a tiny import and then jammed the parking brake on, sliding the huge Suburban's tail-end like a club into the nose of a nearby 18-wheeler. As our training dictated, none of us waited to see if the others were unharmed. We all threw open the door nearest us, sliding out of the belts as quickly as possible and ran for it. The sirens were blaring and close, so close.

A gun barked several times behind me. Tires screeched. People were yelling. I didn't stop to look. My only thoughts were: fence. Over. Junkyard. Hurry. Behind. Behind. Slide through. Go under. Behind. Run. RUN!

After a moment I realized that it was quiet. I stopped my running and stood still. My heart thundered away and my muscles were so wired on adrenaline that my arms twitched. I was surrounded on all sides by piles of old cars fifteen feet high, a huge canyon of crushed and battered old steel. Twenty-foot openings between the walls ran like streets, crossing one another at right angles. It was like a picture of a Grand Canyon I'd seen in a magazine when I was little, only the rows ran impossibly straight. I jogged further down the row to find the door to a building through an opening.

I thought for a moment about going in versus continuing to run when I heard dogs barking and voices. The row ran on straight for quite some distance before it intersected another at a right angle. The dogs would be on me before I could duck around a corner. I stepped forward to try the door and found it unlocked.

I stepped inside.

The door hadn't closed completely when I heard someone yell, "There he is!"

I ran in, my eyes taking a moment to adjust to the darkness. This room was large, empty, and held up by four enormous columns stretching from bare concrete floor to roof. On the far wall was another doorway leading to another room that looked similar, but had a lot of debris and discarded machinery in it.

"Cover," I said to myself.

Just as I began running for the door on the far wall, the door behind me opened. I wanted to look back, but my training said not to. I ran for the door, firing a few unaimed shots behind me. Rifles barked behind me and something searing hot tore through my right calf as I made the far doorway and dove over and behind a large gray cabinet.

"So," I said to myself, "this is where it's going to happen."

File 2618-69370-B

Final Report Prisoner #9370-B

Per orders of Judge Thomas Rorty, Prisoner #9370-B, otherwise known as Marcus Rudenko, was injected with lethal chemicals at 08:26 on 14 October 2015. Subject was pronounced dead 12 minutes later. As per order of General Nathan Westhousen, prisoners remains were immediately cremated, and no attempt was made to collect the ashes.

End of File

AARON

I was trying to remember if I'd called my mom recently and also trying to keep my head while the room spun around me. Night pressed close against the windows outside. The room was lit up and full of bodies but not nearly as loud as it would normally have been. I felt like they were all watching me. It wasn't as awkward as it could have been, though; they were my lovers, and I was theirs. I'd been with all of them in one way or another. I knew their names, their sounds, the way they slept curled against one another. I'd had them inside me, swallowed them, and they me in return.

They were mine. I was theirs. In that moment, high and drunk, I felt connected.

"Aaron," Marcus said, stepping over to me and putting his hand on my shoulder. I tried to stand but couldn't. The people around me smiled and laughed in a way that made me feel known and warm. "The time has come," he said. All other conversation stopped, and everyone put their cups down.

"You are now fully one of us. You are ours and we are yours," he said.

There was a cheer and people smiling.

"The mission is all," he said. Everyone in the room repeated it, including me.

"The mission," Marcus said again, his hand still on my shoulder, "is all. Every single one of us is ready to do what he must to forward the mission. Every. Single. One. And now you are one of us, Aaron. Are you ready to do what you must?"

"I am," I said and the room erupted in cheers. People raised their glasses toward me. They smiled and said my name.

"Are you prepared to do what you must to further the cause?" Marcus asked louder.

"I am!" I said. Again, cheers. The energy in the room was intense.

"Do you love us?" Marcus asked much quieter, putting both his hands on my shoulders and pressing himself against me.

"I do," I said, my eyes rolling back in my head. The laughter in the room was coupled with sighs and guttural moans, as if they were all feeling the same thing I was feeling.

"Do we love Aaron?" Marcus asked.

The room came forward and I was embraced. Arms from all directions circled me. Lips were on my neck, my cheeks, my arms, my wrists, my hands. Time stopped. Sometime later I came back to myself as the hands and arms and lips moved away. They were all standing in a circle still incredibly close, waiting.

"Tomorrow," Marcus said, "Aaron, you will become a hero. Tomorrow, you strike your blow to revenge what has been done. By tomorrow night, the world will know your name."

With that, hands from every direction slowly undressed me and the night collapsed into ecstasy. I was loved, caressed, kissed, licked, sucked, penetrated, penetrating…the only thing that existed was my body and what it was made to feel by hands and lips and tongues. I didn't so much fall asleep that night as pass out from exhaustion.

The next morning, I woke to find everyone still near me, but already dressed.

"Come," Marcus said. "We must get you cleaned up and then get the device strapped to you."

In the bath, which was already waiting and somehow the perfect temperature, I was cleaned. Though there was silence, there were smiles and grins and eyes sparkling. There may have been times when I was a baby that I was this loved, but I couldn't recall them. They cleaned between my toes, between my legs, behind my ears. I was made more clean through washing and through loving touch than I had ever been before. I felt as high as I had been through smoke and liquor when they were done. I stood and they dried me gently with a huge white towel.

They took me to one of the bedrooms and helped me into clothes that weren't mine but fit perfectly. Two of the younger ones even knelt to put boots on me, lacing them up with expressions on their faces as though what they were doing was of deadly seriousness. When they were done and I stood, they all stepped back to look at me. Each, in turn, put his hand on me somewhere and said, "I love you."

Marcus stepped into the room, Viktor just behind him. Marcus put his hand on my shoulder and guided me toward the door. "It's time to go," he said, and we walked down the hallway, passing each of the others in turn. They all caught my eye and I could see admiration and love from each.

"It'll just be a short ride to the building across the street from the church where we have the equipment ready to go. We'll get you strapped in and then you'll step into glory," Marcus said.

We stepped out of the house and into the sun.

CATHOLIC CHURCHES ATTACKED

By Jennifer McMahon

December 16th, 2015

Over 100 people are now dead and 341 injured as a series of churches across the nation are bombed. Officials have yet to release any details, but sources say that all of these attacks were carried out by suicide bombers. We don't have confirmation at this time, but all churches that have been attacked were believed to be performing wedding ceremonies at the time.

You may recall that this is similar to the bombing of St. Augustine church earlier this year. There has been rampant speculation that bombing was carried out by a gay extremist group in retaliation for the slew of new laws passed restricting lesbians, gays, and transgendered people from marrying, adopting, and having workplace protections in the rebirth of the social conservative movement since President Thompson's election six years ago.

Representatives have not officially connected these bombings to that earlier incident, but when asked, an inside source did say that the attacks were "eerily similar."

www.ingramcontent.com/pod-product-compliance
Lightning Source LLC
LaVergne TN
LVHW091117080826
845145LV00008B/1951

* 9 7 8 1 6 0 8 6 4 1 7 2 7 *